Finches of Mars

By the same author from The Friday Project

Life in the West
Forgotten Life
Remembrance Day
Somewhere East of Life

-

The Brightfount Diaries
Bury my Heart at W. H. Smiths
Dracula Unbound
Frankenstein Unbound
Moreau's Other Island
The Primal Urge
Brothers of the Head
The Zodiacal Planet Galaxy
The Complete Short Stories: The 1950s

And available exclusively as ebooks

50 x 50: The Mini-sagas
The Horatio Stubbs Trilogy
The Squire Quartet
The Monster Trilogy

BRIAN ALDISS

Finches of Mars

The Friday Project
An imprint of HarperCollins*Publishers*
77–85 Fulham Palace Road
Hammersmith, London W6 8JB

www.harpercollins.co.uk

First published in Great Britain by The Friday Project in 2013

1

A catalogue record for this book
is available from the British Library

ISBN: 978-0-00-747892-7

Typeset in Minion by
Palimpsest Book Production Ltd, Falkirk, Stirlingshire

Printed and bound in Great Britain by
Clays Ltd, St Ives plc

MIX
Paper from
responsible sources
FSC www.fsc.org **FSC C007454**

For my grandsons
in the future
Laurence and Thomas
(Thomas who was the first person
to read this discourse)
And to Jason and Max
and Ben and of course
Archie
with my love.

He who can read Sir Charles Lyell's grand work on the *Principles of Geology*, which the future historian will recognise as having produced a revolution in natural science, and yet does not admit how vast have been the past periods of time, may at once close this volume.

– Charles Darwin,
*On the Origin of Species by Means of Natural Selection,
or, the Preservation of Favoured Races in the Struggle for Life*

Your idea regarding the effect of gravity on foetal development is absolutely fascinating, and is of much interest to me . . .

There is a great deal of knowledge in the field of foetal development about the importance of physical distorting forces on inducing foetal growth, making your idea of "lighter gravity" affecting foetal life entirely feasible (and to the best of my knowledge absolutely original to boot). Further, the effect of changes of gravity on heart action and blood flow is also fascinating, especially since the foetus is not as well equipped as is its mother.

So, malformed foetuses being at risk of dying in utero or at birth is a plausible conjecture.

Professor Frank Manning
Division of Maternal Foetal Medicine
New York Medical College
New York

FINCHES OF MARS

All those who prefer to whatever degree the hypothetical over what is called reality, finding the real so deplorable that they seek out what may never be, will find here elements for enjoyment. Those optimists who grieve over the shortcomings of existence may like to imagine that better prospects will be created in the future, not least amid the airless deserts of Mars depicted here.

1

An Oceanless World

The word 'scenery' was not in use on Mars. One might talk instead of 'the prospect'.

The prospect was modestly dramatic. Volcanoes on this section of Tharsis were small and scattered. The settlement site on the Tharsis Shield had been chosen for its underground water supply and its comparative smoothness. A path had been worn leading eastwards a short way. A man and woman were walking side-by-side along the path, treading with the high-kneed gait the lower gravity of Mars encouraged. The pair were thickly dressed and wore face masks, since they were beyond the atmospheric confine of the project settlement.

This constitutional exercise, though remarkable enough, had come about by events and arrangements of some complexity, inspired in large part by the findings of the NASA experimental vehicle, *Curiosity*, in 2012AD – when both of these new Martians were not even conceived.

Rooy and Aymee were taking their daily exercise. They had discovered in the austerities of this derelict planet something they had sought without success in their previous lives. No air: perfect vision – clarity of sight and mind. Martian orange-grey sterility. Aymee, dark of skin and outspoken, always declared that Mars served as a physical manifestation of the support system of the subconscious.

The great spread of an oceanless world surrounded them. Such water as there was flowed hidden underground. As usual, the couple had walked until the brow of Olympus Mons showed like consciousness above the horizon

They were walking now between two volcanoes, believed to be extinct, Pavonis Mons and, to the south, Arsia Mons, passing quite close to the rumpled base of the former. In one of these small fissures they had found a little clump of cyanobacteria which added to the interest of their walk. They believed it to be a mark of an ancient underground waterway.

Their progress was slow; Rooy had his left leg encased in plaster, setting a broken bone.

Little Phobos, having risen in the west, was at present speeding above the Shield. Sight of it was obscured by a wind that carried fine dust. The dust and the distant star, Sol, low on the landscape, gave a dull golden aspect to everything.

'I was wondering about our contentment,' Aymee said. 'If we weren't under some odd compulsion to come here? Or if we're not here and are experiencing some form of delusion? Reality can be rather tenuous up here.'

'And not only here,' said Rooy, chuckling.

Back on Earth, one of the screamers had run an opinion poll about the six towers in the Martian settlement. The towers were graded as follows:

CHINESE: MOST ELABORATE
WEST: MOST LEARNED
RUSS-EAST: MOST ARTISTIC
SINGA-THAI: MOST EXCLUSIVE
SCAND: MOST SPARTAN
SUD-AM: MOST EXOTIC

'Maybe there's something to be said for making it up as you go along,' said Aymee. 'How do "they" know what it feels like to be here?'

'It's nice to know we're still in the news, however conjectural.'

'Conjectural? More like a sideshow.'

'I wake up every morning to marvel,' said Rooy.

'And sleep every evening to snore.'

'Was it the twentieth century author, someone Burgess, who said, "Laugh and the world laughs with you, snore and you snore alone."?'

'Anthony, I believe. Anyhow, you've told me that one before.'

They fell silent. Something in the ambience of the prospect, engendered silence. Some found this ambience alarming, some a delight – if a delight of an uncertain kind.

It was Rooy who spoke next.

'You know what I miss most?' he said. 'Rajasthan.'

'Rajasthan!' Aymee exclaimed. She had been born there of a high caste Hindu family. 'Parts of Tharsis remind me of parts of Rajasthan.'

She thought only of the sandy reaches, where the odd goat might be found, and not of the fecund regions where deer ran and rutted among acacia trees.

The West tower loomed ahead of them. It did not stand alone. All told, the six towers had been built within sight of each other: not close enough to form an illusion of 'togetherness', yet still near enough to each other to make, as it might be, a statement of intent – that humanity had arrived at last, and was trying to form something more than a mere voice crying in the wilderness.

And those voices . . . The UU had created linguistic rather than political bases for each site.

A number of pipes led in from the wilds into the basement of the West's building; the water they carried had been charted by Operation Horizon over a year previously. Methane plumes escaping from under the planetary crust were trapped to serve heating and cooking requirements. This development, as with the towers themselves, and the whole Mars enterprise, was funded by the UU. The settlement thus remained ever dependent on terrestrial liberality.

Liberality. Something else absorbed into the unceasing terrestrial power struggle: a tap easily turned off.

Confronting the grey tower, Rooy said, 'Back to the subterranean life . . .' He was a machinist and spent much of his life underground.

Once Aymee and Rooy were inside the confinement zone they could remove their masks and breathe shallowly. In a year or two – or maybe three – the modest area of contained atmosphere would have approached normal limits. The six towers stood in this zone under a large friction-stir welding dome; from this leaked an atmosphere consisting mainly of nitrogen, mixed with 21.15% oxygen. The circular zone guard retained most of the gas. Still, few people cared to stay unmasked outside the towers for long.

As Aymee punched in their code, she said, 'Another new word needed there. "Subterranean" can't be right.'

The gate was opened by the door guardian, a man called Phipp, who hustled the pair in. Guardianship was considered to be an important post. Blood, pulse and eyesight readings had to be taken by automatic machines within the martial confinement of the gatehouse before anyone from outside was allowed to move freely inside.

This entailed a delay of only 55 seconds, unless the automatics detected reasons for stoppage and possible treatment; nevertheless this precautionary delay was widely resented. Resented, although Mars imposed its own delay on the passage of time. Aymee and Rooy waited at the tower gate, hand in hand.

2

A Freedom

'*Sub specie aeternitatis* – that's us,' said Noel, who had been elected more or less as Director of the West tower. 'We have "*aeternitatis*" all round us in trumps. Our function is to occupy – what? – emptiness. And to discuss those abstract and vital questions that have vexed humanity since . . . well, since the first human-like babe fell out of a vague quaternary tree. Who would like to kick off?'

The woman to whom a terrestrial computer had allotted the name Sheea said, 'Are we the elite or the rejects, Noel?'

Noel raised a delicate eyebrow. 'I prefer to think of us as the elite.'

'Here we are on Tharsis Shield, parked in six towers – we were so proud of being chosen for this extraordinary exile – is this indeed the honour we imagine it to be? Or do you think we have been dumped here so as not to interfere with the villainies brewing on Earth?'

'Not a question you can usefully ask,' said Noel. She spoke lightly, knowing Sheea faced the challenges of pregnancy.

*   *   *

The possibilities of a wise and peaceful terrestrial future had been destroyed by vicissitudes of fortune and the accidents of history. Only occasionally on the planet Earth do we find a nation at peace with itself and its neighbours. The quest for happiness – in itself not a particularly noble occupation – has in general been overcome by a lust for riot and slaughter. Violent and vengeful nations have arisen, seething with illiterates enslaved by ancient writings.

The more peevish the nation, the more primitive its preaching.

Occasionally one finds states where all seems quiet and without disturbance; these in the main prove to be police states, where disagreement is ruthlessly suppressed, and only the most powerful have freedom of movement to a limited degree.

On the planet Mars it is different.

But of course Mars is not over-populated.

The human settlement on Mars has its share of human woes. But here for once sagacity prevails, perhaps because the occupants of the various towers are so few, and have been so carefully selected.

Noel in her bed at night thinks always of the great Mangalian.

These chosen persons living on the Shield must succeed or die. They have signed a contract making it impossible for them to return to the planet from which, in either the name of advancement or adventure, they have voluntarily exiled themselves.

Many small restrictions apply here. Nothing may be wasted, not even human dung. No pets at all may be kept in the towers. Recreational drugs are not available, and may not be used if found.

The scarcity of oxygen and the increased distance from a volatile sun may contribute to the stability of the Martian venture. The mentality of these exiles, as we shall see, has been liberated by their freedom from belief in the dictates of an inscrutable god.

3

Mangalian's Remark

To be on Mars . . .

This almost evolutionary step owes its existence to a small group of learned and wise men and women. Working at the end of the previous century, and spurred on to begin with by the provocation of the great Herbert Amin Saud Mangalian, the universities of the cultivated world linked themselves together under a charter which in essence represented a great company of the wise, the UU (for United Universities). The despatch of the two hydrologists to our nearby planet was the first UU move.

Mangalian spent a profligate youth on San Salvador, the island in the Bahamas, fathering several children with several women. The edict 'Go forth and multiply' was his inspiration. Only when he met and married Beth Gul – both taking delight in this antiquated ceremony – did he reform, encouraged by her loving but disputatious nature. For a while he and Beth severed their connections with others. They read and studied; they led a rapt hermit's life.

Together, the two of them wrote a book from which great consequences sprang. It was entitled *The Unsteady State or, Starting Again from Scratch.*[1] As was the fashion, this volume contained moving video and screamer shots married into the text. It argued that humanity on Earth was doomed, and that the only solution was to send our best away, where they could strive – on Mars and beyond – to achieve true civilization. It was sensationalist, but persuasive.

The declaration alarmed many in the West and infuriated many more in the Middle-East, as is generally the way when truth is plainly stated. It brought Mangalian to public attention.

He was an attractive young fellow, tall, sinewy, with a mop of jet black hair – and a certain gift of the gab.

It was only after his remark, 'Countless lungs, countless penises, all working away! We shall run out of oxygen before we run out of semen!' that Mangalian's name became much more widely known, and his book more attentively read. 'Semen is always trendy,' he told an interviewer, by way of explanation.

'A handsome fellow,' was how many people expressed in their various languages admiration and envy of Mangalian. Using his book as both inspiration and guide, several intellectuals made tentative efforts to link universities as the first step towards civilization elsewhere. There was no doubt that Mangalian was a vital advocate for a new association – the UU. While there were many who enthused over the idea of the UU, almost as many – in the main those living in slums, tents and sink estates – raged against its exclusivity.

So Mangalian, a youth with no university degree, became head, figurehead, of the newly formed UU. He was aware that any sunshine of global attention had its rapid sunset. Invited to England, he attracted representatives from the three leading universities, to shower them with challenges to unite.

'All know you to be a footballing nation, but Q.P.R. and Q.E.D.[2]

---

[1] A brief synopsis of this book can be found at the end of this text.
[2] Queens Park Rangers. A football team. Quod erat demonstrandum. Latin conclusion of proof.

should not be adversarial. A ball in the net is great – so is the netting of new facts.' He was being facile, but his argument scored a goal. The first three universities raised the purple and blue flag of the UU.

But a left wing politician remarked, 'So, the words come from Oxford, but the cash comes from China . . .' It was certainly true, although not widely admitted, that NASA projects were nowadays kept afloat on Beijing currency – it was unlikely to be little different with the UU.

Under the goading of the young impresario Mangalian, many universities agreed to join the first three, to create a nation-like body of new learning, a corpus aloof from the weltering struggles of an underfed, under-educated and unreasoning range of random elements: the sick, the insane, the suicide-bombers and their like. Mangalian disliked this division. It was then he spoke for the colonisation of Mars. MARS, he said, stood for 'MANKIND ACHIEVING (a) RENEWED SOCIETY.' Some laughed, some jeered. But the movers at last moved.

Even before all the various universities had finished signing on their various dotted United lines, an exploration duo was sent out to inspect Martian terrain. The terrain had been photographed previously, but trodden by a human's boot – never.

Operation Horizon consisted of two men and a robotruck. Modest though this expedition was, the future of an entire enterprise depended on it. If no watercourses were detected, then the great UU initiative was sunk as surely as the *Titanic*; if water was detected, and in sufficient quantities, then the project would proceed. Everything depended on two skilled hydrologists and a new-fangled robotruck, designed especially for the task.

The truck could be spoken to by screamer from a kilometre's distance. It was loaded with equipment. It also gave two men shelter in the chill sleep hours, and enabled them to refill their oxygen tanks.

While electronics experts and eager young engineers worked on the truck, various hydrology experts were being interviewed. One of the men given the okay was the experienced Robert Prestwick, fifty-six years of age, and the other Henry Simpson, sixty-one years old, famous for his design of the dome over Luna. He wasn't just a skilled hydrologist. Prestwick was a heavily built, blue jowled man. Simpson was of slighter build, and a head shorter than his friend. The robotruck was new, as stated.

The hydrologists had known each other on and off for roughly thirty years, having first met at Paranal Observatory in Chile, which had been temporarily beset by flood problems. Now they joked, 'So they send us to a planet believed to be without water . . .'

It seemed to be that way at first. The two men had begun by surveying the great central feature of the Martian globe, the Valles Marinaris, a gash in the planet a mile deep, stretching for almost two thousand miles. Howling winds blowing along the rift from east to west carried dust storms with them. The gales blew along its uninviting length, persuading the men to choose a more promising area to the north. The robotruck took them to the Tharsis Shield – at the north of which stood the grand old extinct volcano, Olympus Mons, once believed to be the home of gods. If their exploration was successful, no one believing in God was to be allowed on Mars.

Henry Simpson grumbled at the dimness of the light. 'It's like 4.30 on a December afternoon back home. Midnight, in other words.'

'Don't complain,' said Prestwick, with a chuckle. 'At least God has given us this spare planet for gainful employment . . . We're sniffing water!' He pointed to the screen, his mood changed entirely. The robotruck was moving slowly; a flickering vein of green showed on its screen. They halted, getting a depth check.

'Nine point four feet below surface.'

Prestwick wondered to himself what it would be like to have to live here. He'd been to some bleak places back home. Here, there was nothing but bleakness, water or no water . . .

Simpson came and stared over his comrade's shoulder at the screen.

'Okay! Good! We need something nearer surface, but without being frozen solid.'

On the sweep again, they watched green delta-like traces close into a single strip. It then become faint and vanished. Simpson scratched his head.

'We've struck an area.' He spoke surprisingly calmly.

Stopping the machine, Prestwick asked, 'Retrace?'

'Hang on. There's still something . . .' Simpson had what they called a dedeaf to his forehead. Faintly came an intermittent boom and a faint low plop, such as a leaky tap might make, dripping into a puddle. The noises faded away and then returned, the tap noise slightly louder now.

'Something's going on. Can only be water.' Simpson shivered. The sound was not a friendly one. 'Couldn't be horse piss,' he added.

Prestwick by now had a dedeaf to his forehead too. He pulled a face at his partner. Both were well aware they were isolated on an unfriendly planet and this discovery would extend their stay. It was a disappointment – another week finding nothing and they would have been on the way back home. In time for Christmas. However, it was a well-paid stretch of employment.

'Go on a bit,' Simpson told the truck. 'Slowly, okay?'

They growled onwards, watching the screen. Suddenly the green strip was back on screen. It fattened. A thin green vein ran off from it, disappearing at the side of the screen. The sound too had changed; the dedeafs brought a noise as of someone humming tunelessly in a deep voice.

The strip widened, becoming marrow-shaped.

'Depth down to surface?' Simpson asked.

'Nineteen point nine to surface,' reported the truck.

He sighed. 'And to bottom?'

'Twenty-eight . . . correction . . . twenty-nine to bottom.'

The two men exchanged glances.

'Small reservoir? Not bad.'

'Better mark it. We can map the extent later.'

They climbed out and stood there on the lee side of the truck until the truck extruded a coloured peg containing internal figures which could be read by any other truck, should such a thing ever come this way.

It was a melancholy thought. The expedition was no more than that. Nothing might ever come this way again. Simpson shuddered inside his uniform.

The hydrologists laid a track. When a map was drawn up, a spider-like effect was apparent, with small streams leading off a reservoir of considerable size. The men were neither pleased nor displeased. Instead, they decided to take a rest.

'We're not as young as we were – even you,' said Prestwick.

'You're kidding,' said Simpson.

It was a struggle to climb into the small bunk beds. They slept in their clothes – breathing masks, boots and all. Simpson went outside, peering over the roof of the truck. Mars was like an old black-and-white illustration, such as one saw in the bygone newspapers of the early Twentieth Century. A few shapes, mysterious and malign, stood here and there – emblems of a cosmic disorder. Some distance ahead of Simpson stood his wife, Katie, motionless.

Simpson called to her, but sound did not carry. As he moved towards her, his boots grew heavier. He thought some white thing drifted above him, but could not raise his head to look.

'My God, it's lovely here!' – he had meant to say 'lonely' rather than 'lovely'. 'It's the graveddy,' he told himself. 'Makes the lippers frabby.'

Olympus Mons lay somewhere ahead of him. Like a tit. Katie's tit.

'Katie!' he called. Defying the laws of perspective, she became smaller as he approached. Her head was pointed. She had no face. She wore a trailing frock. He broke into a run. 'Wait! Wait!'

She did not move. She dripped.

Katie was simply an icy pinnacle. A rocky spike adorned with a garment of multiple frosts. A thing to be hated rather than loved.

'Oh, don't do this,' Simpson begged.

He looked round in despair. The world was empty. High above, a tiny distant spark moved.

'You must be Swift . . . Named by Jonathan Deimos.' He spoke in a whisper. He had enlisted for this venture to escape his loneliness after his wife's death. But here it was echoing with loneliness: a whole planet full of it . . .

He found himself looking about, eyes half closed, dreading to see something, nothing. His wife would never visit Mars. This was a place of which God had never heard. So it had remained vacant and unwanted. Up For Sale. He fell to his knees.

It was impossible to say how greatly his way of life had changed since Kate had died.

He lay in a kind of paralysis. Absurd to say he did not care about Kate; absurd not to say how much more . . . interesting . . . life had become.

Suppose it *had* been Katie just now and *he* who was dying. Dying in the snow . . .

Prestwick was leaning over him. He asked, 'You all right, mate?'

Simpson returned to consciousness as if from the depths of an ocean. 'What a dream! What a hellish place Mars is! Why should anyone want to come and live here? It's like a fucking cemetery.'

Prestwick remarked on the noise Simpson had been making, and advised him to take another sleeping pill, before changing the subject. 'Do you remember when astronomers thought there was a major planet out beyond Pluto? Then they said it didn't exist, but instead there was a planet they called Eris. They'll be trying to get to Eris next. It's beyond the Kuiper Belt.'

Simpson made nothing of this, his mind being still filled with the sludge of his dream. 'Jesus, I could do with a drink. The bastards might have granted us a bottle of rum.'

'Ah, but rum costs. The bastards didn't send us here to drink.'

'Sodding teetotallers, that's what . . .'

Silence fell between them until Prestwick pressed a button on the robotruck. 'Get us two coffees, will you?'

'Coming up.'

When Prestwick spoke again, he sounded rather tentative. 'They are certainly paying us well enough for this job. I'm still paying off putting my two boys through college. But there have always been aspects of this job I hate.

'For instance, if this UU project goes through, religion on the planet will be banned. Anyone getting here will have to be atheists.'

'They can give the place to the devil for all I care.'

Prestwick hunched himself up in his bunk. 'No, look, I want to talk seriously. We've got on okay. Now I'm a bit older, I start to try to think more deeply. Needs, regrets, desires . . . The way the impression section of your brain works. As a youngster, I was always too busy getting laid. Remember when we first met in Chile? I picked up – or I was picked up by – a woman who called herself Carmen. It was intended to be a one-night stand, but somehow we got a liking for each other. It was

13

odd. Suddenly from impersonal to personal. She had a nice laugh.' He was thinking, *No one as yet has ever laughed on Mars . . .*

'Carmen! I'd do anything for a laugh in those days. I caught a rickety old coach out to her place. She held my hand with her rough hand. My hand so smooth – two worlds meeting – I felt a bit ashamed. Anything foreign excited me. I always had a hard on.

'Carmen lived in a little village outside Santiago. She'd come into the city *pro tem* because she heard there were foreigners visiting and she thought that a bit of whoring could raise some necessary cash. So it did. But her place . . . She was dog poor, poor darling. She lived in one room and next door was a sort of lean to – a stall with a corrugated iron roof where she kept a little cart and a donkey on a tether.'

'You and your memories!' Simpson scoffed. 'At least it's better than you moaning about the constipation, and your sodding painful testicles!'

'I can't tell you how excited I was to be there with her. This was the real world – even to the extent that I got a mild dose of the clap off her. We slept on cushions. She had had a bloke, but he had left her directly the baby was born. Her ma looked after the kiddie when Carmen was away. And she fed the donkey. Her old mum knew what bastards men could be.

'Carmen took it all in her stride. Massive good nature. Heavy but neat little tits with stretch marks. She expected men to be shits who would leave their women to make out and bring up the kids. She worked hard as a carrier with her little donkey cart . . . Oh, sorry, Henry, I've got carried away, going on like this. It was just such a – oh, a rich experience.'

'I wonder what percentage of women live more or less as Carmen did. There are plenty worse places than Santiago,' said Simpson.

'The way she looked at you when you woke in the morning. Eyes like a lioness . . . Christ, I should stop this. I'm going on for sixty – not a kid any more. But some women you never forget.'

'Go ahead,' said Simpson, yawning. 'I had rather a posh hotel tart when we were in Santiago. Delicious in bed, but she meant nothing to me. Warm enough inside but cold outside.'

The coffee arrived in two small sealed plastic cups.

14

'The point I'm getting at,' said Prestwick, as he sipped the flavour-less liquid, 'is that Carmen knew nothing. She knew nothing of all this vast heap of cleverness we know all too well. The whole urban thing. Yet she knew so much we don't know. When there would be an hour's electricity, where the river water ran pure, how the old donkey was feeling today, how you mended an axle, how to shit and piss without giving offence, how to have a little fire without burning the fucking place down, how to bake . . . oh, a thousand things. All to do with survival. How to keep in with the priest. A priest whom I met, by the way. Priests are always ill-spoken of, but this priest was a real holy man. He'd help if Carmen had a spot of trouble with the donkey's hooves, for instance.

'If Carmen or her ma complained, he'd say, "Never mind, Jesus got himself crucified for less . . ."'

'I had a chance to talk with this priest. His name was Festa, or so I seem to remember. You see, I still recall it after all these years. He said that men were fools. They did not respect women, the givers of life. He said there were some women who had special qualities. He named Carmen as an example. He said, there was a comfort – that was his word – a comfort when you thought about her. Not sexual attraction, because as a priest he should not experience sexual attraction. But even when she was away, still that feeling of comfort.

'Comfort. We were drinking the local wine. He said, this priest said, without thinking, that sometimes he woke in the night and burned with desire for Carmen. I was sleeping with her. I knew well what the poor fellow meant . . .'

Prestwick paused.

'But after all, so many women . . .' He let the sentence trail away into the godless night. 'I felt we'd got it wrong – the West. I mean, got it wrong.' He lapsed into silence.

'I make it sound as if I lived in that village for years. I was only there for two days. I didn't like the rats. We've gotten so squeamish. But somehow Carmen – really the whole place, I guess – it started working on my mind.'

Simpson said, simply, 'I envy you.'

'Carmen . . .' Silence fell between them, except for the sipping noises.

'I see what you mean,' said Simpson eventually. 'Yes. The place sounds like a film set. *The Simple Life*. But what if you get ill? Or your kids? And her ex – miserable slob. Did she get the clap attended to?'

'I couldn't live there. Nor could you, I imagine. I got my dose cleared up back home.'

Simpson was reluctant to enter into further conversation. 'Let's switch the recorder off, shall we?' he suggested, but hesitated as Prestwick continued, undeterred.

'I couldn't – we couldn't live in Chile. Ghastly place, ghastly politics, to be honest. We owe a whole heap to the Magna Carta. But just think of the world we do live in. We're inculcated, if that's the word I want. Inculpated? Our minds – well, look, as far as we know our brains were jerry-built over the ages from brains of – crikey! – brains of sea monsters – sea monsters and then, later, a form of ape. And for all endeavours–'

Simpson groaned. 'Stop it right there, Bob. I'm sick of being told we've all come down from the trees. We are no longer apes and there's the difference. Did you ever meet an ape who was a hydrologist? A president of a bank, okay, but not a hydrologist.'

'No, no, I wasn't off on that tack, mate. I was going to say that, thanks to Charles Darwin and others, we have been released from the Old Testament. I rejoice in that. We came from simple villagers, believing Earth was the centre of the universe. The prospects of evolution are far more thrilling than almost any other theory ever dreamed up . . .

'But . . . we seem still to need faith. A faith. Any faith. And I suspect our brains – urh! the brains of modern man – are stacked full of an erroneous faith. Office bumf . . . Faith in information. Information about everything, anything. Its birthday may have been the dropping of the atomic bomb on Japan, way back when.

'Since about then, we have craved to know . . . quantum theory, mass, energy, time, space, neurons, protons, DNA, cosmology, geology, the credit card, the simple screamer. All bits of information sprawling about our desks. These constitute our faith. God the Father, God the Son, etc., have been banished in favour of – what, exactly? Well, the Economy, the godless, thankless Economy . . .

16

'And like the faithful anywhere, any time, we don't realise how much it all costs to the human spirit.

'Carmen – a Catholic, she was paying with the clap. So are we, mental clap, exile on Mars . . .'

'You're ranting,' Simpson wanted to say, but refrained.

Henry Simpson was unaccustomed to discussions of this kind. It was true that after the death of his wife he had gone less frequently to the golf club and more often to an art club, where all kinds of matters were discussed, but he was still reluctant to enter into argument with Prestwick. He said, in a way that seemed feeble even to himself, 'But we have so many advantages. I was beginning to suffer from Alzheimer's, but it was cured. We've put the past behind us for present advantages, surely . . .'

'You don't like talking about the past, just as you don't like the thought of being descended from apes?'

Simpson was beginning to feel strained. He spoke with some anger. 'I read novels of the present day. I doubt if I'd read a novel of the Tenth Century, even if there was such a thing.'

Prestwick produced a paperback of an old-fashioned kind and pressed his light to burn brighter.

'Henry, would you mind if I read you a bit of something? It's a life of a woman of the Twelfth Century, written later, after her death. I brought it with me although I've read it a coupla times before. It fascinates me because the lives it depicts are so different from ours of today, and yet both different and similar. It's the life of a woman who became known as Christina of Markyate.'

'I may fall asleep,' Simpson warned.

'Don't worry. I shall kick you if you do. This young lady who became known as Christina lived her life as a virgin. Different from today, different from my Carmen. Anyhow, that's what she did, what she was determined to do. She became a "Bride of Christ". Not that he ever seemed to take a blind bit of notice of her.

'She was a bright girl, her parents were as difficult as could be, in quite a modern way. So this modest and deeply religious girl became betrothed to one Beorhtred. She had been tricked and openly swore she would not be defiled by Beorhtred's carnal embraces. Not likely today!

17

'Her father drags her before the Prior, who asks, "Why should you bring this dishonour to your parents?"'

Simpson looked out into the Martian darkness, where stars burned, and kept silent.

'Christina's answers are splendid; she says to the Prior, "You who are supposed to excel in the knowledge of scripture, must judge how wicked a thing this would be, should my parents enter me into a marriage I never wanted, and make me unfaithful to Christ, He who knows of the vow I had made in my childhood."'

Stifling a yawn, Simpson said, 'She may speak well, as you say, but those were lives lived on false premises. All very well for the Twelfth Century, not now.'

'What I'm trying to argue is that, yes, the premises were false, but no less false are the premises of today. Shall I continue?' Prestwick tweaked a page.

'Her parents, as the book says, "did not know how to see beyond worldly possessions". That has a contemporary ring about it, wouldn't you say? But at every instant, despite the cruelty of her parents, she remained, as she always said a "Bride of Christ". A virgin, in fact.'

'Nowadays, she would have treatment for frigidity,' said Simpson, with a grin. 'Jesus, it's uncomfortable here. You can't even scratch your arse on this bunk.'

'Yes, and these days her parents would be judged guilty of violence against their daughter. But the daughter would nevertheless be harmed. We read of such cases in the screamers every day.'

'Well, cut it short. What happened then?'

'Bad bishops have never been a novelty. With the assistance of one of them, Beorhtred gained power over her. He jeered at Christina in his hour of triumph. She asked him a question. "Tell me, Beorhtred, and may God have mercy on you, if another were to come and take me away from you and marry me, what would you do?" To which he replied in brutish fashion, "I wouldn't put up with it for a moment as long as I lived. I would kill him with my own hands if there were no other way of keeping you."

'So she replies – I love this – she replies, "Beware then of wanting to take to yourself a Bride of Christ, lest in His anger He slay you."'

Simpson gave a laugh. 'She was quick-witted at least. But "Bride of Christ" . . .? Who'd believe that today?'

Prestwick answered sadly, 'No one would. Today most teenage girls in the West have lost their virginity by the age of fifteen and think well of themselves for having done so.'

'So I suppose your Christina went to live in a nunnery . . .'

'Where else would she have gone for safety in those days? Or now?'

Silence fell between the two men. Then Simpson said. 'At least we treat women better now.'

He felt he had scored a point there.

Operation Horizon delivered a positive report to the executive council of the United Universities. Subterranean channels had been charted, and a reservoir containing plentiful H_2O of unknown quality. A map of the area on the Tharsis Shield accompanied their report, with waterways depicted like blue veins.

It was the verdict of the two hydrologists making the report that this area would be a suitable site for the settlement to be established, at least as far as water supply was concerned.

This report provided the necessary impetus for the development of this great and unprecedented enterprise – the colonisation of Mars.

A surveyor by name Moses Barrin was immediately hired to draw up sites for proposed Martian settlements known as towers. His instructions were to demarcate a site where six small habitations could be established. He used maps created from data from both Operation Horizon and even the now ancient NASA vehicle *Curiosity*. Barrin was to be among the first humans sent to colonize Mars.

The Message, newspaper of the Vatican, warned of the moral dangers of venturing onto a planet where Jesus Christ had never trod.

Several screamers showed cartoons of Jesus wandering alone, asking, 'Where's someone to save?'

4
Final Journey

The report of Martian water running underground did much to excite public interest in the project, and to stir the involvement of the universities. There was less talk of trips to Mars being 'madness'. In Chinese cities new factories were manufacturing 'space planes'.

The United Universities, from the original three, had expanded to thirty-one signatories, consisting mainly of universities or departments of universities situated in the United States of America, Britain, Europe and China. Other universities were drawn in as by a magnet, tempted in the main by the two hydrologists' positive report on Tharsis.

Soon there existed a world-wide body of growing strength and ubiquity which stood in defiance of what the British Foreign Minister had described as 'the New Dark Ages of Technofrolic'. After renewed Beijing scrutiny, the charter was revised with fresh restrictions: In addition to the ban on any proposed traveller to Mars with a known religious background, there were to be no travellers above forty-five years old (with certain rare exceptions). Signing members guaranteed to supply regular six-monthly contributions to a central fund. In exchange, signatories were entitled to receive directly any fresh scientific discoveries from Mars.

The news of the hydrologists' discovery had travelled faster than their ship. The names of Simpson and Prestwick were already forgotten by the media by the time the automatic call sign on their tiny returning ship sounded at Luna Lookout. Luna signalled the vessel to come in.

No reply was received.

An emergency ship was sent up. This space plane had been manufactured in nine days in the city of Chenggong, an urban development of forty-nine million people.

The *Aquabatic*, with its freight of the two hydrologists, was gaining speed, heading towards the Sun. The rescuers locked on to its hull, sending a sequence of calls to those within. They went unanswered.

A request for instruction was sent to Lookout. Lookout signalled Chicago-Emergency. Chicago advised immediate entry of ship by men in emergency equipment.

A hole was cut in the *Aquabatic*'s hull and a man by the name of Will Donovan, suitably masked, forced his way in. There he found the bodies of the two hydrologists lying in the cramped living quarters, Prestwick on his bunk, Simpson sprawled face-down on the floor. Both men had been dead for several weeks.

A discolouring heliotrope showed on their skins and faces. An argument was conducted between ship and ground station; the bodies ought to be left where they were, to make their final journey into the Sun undisturbed – the public must not be alarmed by these unanticipated deaths. Alternatively, the bodies should be encapsulated and brought to Hospital Luna under conditions of secrecy, for research purposes.

This was the view that won the day. The corpses were transferred to the rescue ship. Remaining behind to be forever lost were recordings of their vellicative memories. The *Aquabatic* was left to drift on its course towards the Sun.

22

The mystery illness that had stricken the hydrologists served as a warning that it was not simply from the void that dangers could strike. Humanity carried with it many metabolic organisms that eluded interrogation.

At least the disaster led to more cautious preparation for large vessels attempting the gulfs of space. Any person going aboard was subjected to rigorous medical examination which included a period of quarantine.

A rocket named *Zubrin* was the second piece of UU hardware to cross the approximately 50 million miles to Mars. All launches, including this one, were scheduled to take advantage of the best possible mutual orbits. More advanced than the hydrologists' ship, it carried on board no living thing, only an android robot of some size and strength. The android survived both the flight and the landing, whereupon it proceeded to unload building materials, emergency food rations, and some tanks of oxygen, in preparation for future settlers.

'For my next trick . . .' as the android would have said, had it the wit, *Zubrin* turned itself into a drill and began to drill down through the regolith in the expectation of hitting subterranean water.

All this in preparation for the arrival of human beings, poor frail biological constructs who would need water – and much else besides. Later, later . . . Politics thrives on delays.

First of all, the UU, still developing and having now signed up Moscow University, pursued the programme known as D&D (standing for Distance and Danger). The distance problem was regarded as a ten-month ordeal, sometimes less. It had to be endured between Earth and Mars. New faster space planes were cutting journey times. Humans back in the Paleolithic age had accustomed themselves to dealing with distances, when hunter-gathering enforced ceaseless movement of groups and tribes. The challenge of distances in space was met by the development of a plasma drive, instead of a chemical drive, which made journeys faster and a good deal safer.

There still remained among the dangers exposure to radiation during the journey. Three forms of radiation were known, protons emanating from the Sun, heavy ions from cosmic rays, and the newly discovered normon, radiating from the Oort Cloud. (At this time, the normon was regarded as benevolent, indeed as a helpful propagator of microscopic life on early Earth.)

If shielding were added to the space vehicle it would slow its progress, prolonging time of exposure. Cataracts and cancers would still occur. For at least another century, the visit to Mars was generally regarded as a one-way trip. Only Barrin was to make it both ways.

Still, there were those, and not the most foolhardy either, who spoke out to say it was necessary to leave Earth, an Earth by now riddled, like death watch beetles in old timber, with threats including random procreation (now recognised as another contribution to global warming), new super-bugs, missile systems, and hostile and distraught dictatorial states. Supposing the pioneers *were* to die on Mars: they were already on what Hamlet had termed 'a place from whose bourn no traveller returns!' Corpses would be wrapped in polythene and left to mummify by an outer wall.

The first arrivals, sponsored and supported by UU, found themselves suffering from many lesser maladies which light Martian gravity did little to heal. Brave hearts had had less reason to pump strongly in the weightlessness of the journey. Bones and muscles had been weakened, despite rigorous exercise-routines compulsory on the trip.

Broken bones were frequent – but lo! The miracle! There one stood on the planet Mars – even if only with a crutch! Space anaemics, deficient in red blood cells, vied with the crippled for beds in temporary Martian hospital wards. Even injured, they set machines to building permanent bases, the towers – all under the watchful eye of Barrin.

Six towers now stood on the Tharsis bulge. Some towers were taller than others, some more substantial, depending on UU contributions. There were connections between all of these outposts of humanity and also, inevitably, some mistrust, the dregs of old hostilities. In the settlement, West and Chinese were closest and in friendly communication.

For stay-at-homes, photographs of the half-dozen buildings standing in defiance on the Tharsis Shield were as popular as studies of Earth seen from Moon had once been, or kittens wearing ribbons still were.

5
The Shape of the UU

Mangalian had had a say in the positioning of this, the settlement, and even the universal sale of its photographs. Under his guidance, the UU's Mars enterprise progressed rapidly.

He showed undoubted flair. NASA/Beijing had a stable organisation with a patient professional ability to plan projects which would not come to fruition until years later. The UU formed a union with NASA, and benefitted from this planning. The UU/NASA union instigated a raft of interviews and examinations, dedicated to continuous selection of those of either sex prepared to prove themselves good citizens of a distant planet. Only the educated and adventurous need apply. 'The wise and the wild,' as news shriekers had it.

The Union issued non-return certificates to those whose credentials had been accepted. Many had already taken up their situations in the Tharsis region, in the towers, accepting that there was no return to planet Earth. Potential colonists continued to join.

Only four years later, a dedicated worker from Mangalian's main office, Rosemary Cavendish, went to Mars herself. She adopted the humbler name of Noel. A new department in UU/NASA had suggested that terrestrial names should be replaced by computerised names for use on Mars. It symbolised a new beginning, and a marginal amount of finance would be saved. For a while this system was used, eventually to be abandoned in the face of the confusion it caused. Too many people were rejecting their new name from the start.

Rosemary/Noel had an important role in Mangalian's grand theatre. She was made Director of the West tower immediately after her arrival there.

So the colonisation process continued towards its remarkable outcome.

A few years passed. Bernard Tibbett and his partness Lulan entered the scene. Lulan was a retired President of Harvard University and Bernard Head of Harvard Business School. Tibbett was voted official banker[3] and President of World UU. A short sharp man, he became known for his energies as the Terrier. His partness – a woman intolerant of weakness – was the Grey Wolf. People – 'the great un-castrated' in the Grey Wolf's words – should not mourn at funerals but celebrate – one more over-populator, one more consumer, less.

This forbidding couple had more than money and status invested in the distant Martian Towers. The Terrier had a younger sister, once called Dolores, but now on Mars and renamed Sheea. Sheea, the Terrier learnt, was now pregnant, despite only having been on the planet a few months. Curiously, no name of the inseminator had been given. Good care was being taken of her. Sheea had been moved to stay the West tower gestation ward and was on a special diet. Everyone was hoping for a successful birth.

Tibbett was making a speech when the news that his distant sister was going into labour came through. The Terrier was immediately anxious for his sister's well-being, but had to attend to the meeting.

The delegates were at a regular committee. On this occasion the

---

[3] Here meaning mainly custodian of all wills and ordinances.

honoured guest, Barrin, was attending. Barrin appeared in a wheelchair. He had been on Mars and returned to Earth. The King of England had given him a medal especially coined for the occasion. Barrin vowed to go back to his colleagues on Mars, but his legs were unlikely to permit it. More significant, he was having problems with breathing. His lungs had already been equipped with a chemical pump.

'We of UU,' said Tibbett, stroking his chin and frowning, 'constantly worry about the expense of sustaining the Mars operation. Rightly so. We need better vehicles, more space planes, to carry larger cargoes. We might then be able to drastically reduce the present number of trips, thus keeping to a minimum the number of expensive rockets lying unused on Tharsis. If even a half of the investment spent on military matters – now that the morally unjustified, short-sighted invasion of Kazakhstan and the bombing of Alma Ata is over – was invested in the construction of better space vehicles with more effective propellant systems . . . Well, as you know, experiments are taking place in Chenggong. A prospectus to this effect is already being drawn up.

'We must noise it in the press and the squealers and shriekers, otherwise the news will be suppressed. We are already at the planning stage.'

After a brief coffee break, the Principal of the University of South Africa rose to protest that volunteers for visits to Mars were forced to stay as they would not be allowed to return to Earth. 'This is a punitive feature of the deal. We would have many more volunteers if they could return after, say, a six month stay.'

The delegate from Oxford University responded. 'Those who make the decision to go to Mars must leave Earth as exiles. It would prove impossible to finance such comings and goings as proposed; the expense would defeat our objectives. Besides which, this restriction on movement simply excludes the faint-hearted. We need only the brave and wise to begin habitation. Soon, children, we hope, will be born on Tharsis. They will be the guarantors of our serious intentions.'

A murmur of agreement went round the chamber. Of course – children! Without children, no future, no permanence . . .

But therein lay a tragic history, so far suppressed.

Other matters brought other disputes. Tibbett summed up one of them.

'We applaud the strong measures being taken by our colleagues in South China's universities for their new decision to curb population growth. I know that when Miss Ban Mu Kai takes over my position as president in October, she will support and amplify our recent report on Sub-Saharan Africa, still the region with the most profligate birth rates and lowest average life-spans.'

A woman from the University of Hawaii rose to her feet and protested that much more and not much less should be done to educate the women of Africa.

Tibbett was unmoved. 'Colonial incursions into Africa in the Nineteenth Century only made a bad situation worse.

'It is up to this region to solve its own problems. In the past, millions have been squandered on aid, almost always to zero effect. Throwing money at corruption is worse than useless. Intervention, interference, of any kind, whether criminal or benevolent, should be proscribed, subject to legal penalties.'

At this point there was another word from the floor. Barrin himself raised his hand. 'Sir, I am here from Mars to attend this and other world meetings. My name is Barrin. If I interpret your statement correctly, you encourage the UU to leave Africa to its ills unaided. Against such ruthlessness, it would appear that we of the Mars project also have much to fear in the way of withdrawal of necessary funding.'

'You are welcome here, sir,' said the Terrier, addressing Barrin. 'But your fears are – and I intend no pun – groundless. When the UU established themselves as a group with an identity, the Mars project – suggested by Mangalian and supported by NASA/Beijing – was the very first item on the agenda, and has remained so. And will remain so.

'The success of the UU Mars project is absolutely vital for this troubled planet too.

'I will remind you and everyone here that we were prompted into our existing unification by the continuing increase in population figures. The global population has been increasing since as far back as 1350, but it has only been in the last century, with better medical care and longer fertility, that it has become frightening – truly unbearable. We are living crushed together, stacked on top of each other. Existence has become miserable. As our colleague, Lee Kuan Shi, remarked – an oft-quoted saying – "We gotta get outta here!"'

A ripple of pleasure passed through the audience on hearing this old refrain. During the days when the pressure to establish the Mars base was at its most fervent, 'We gotta get outta here!' became a slogan that helped win the day.

Addressing Barrin directly, Tibbett said, 'We will schedule your preliminary report for the afternoon session. You will be able to speak at 4 p.m.'

He then continued with his main summary. 'Problems are mounting up. The USA's UU Bureau of Statistics reports an increase in the incursions of super-bugs, widespread food shortages and lack of drinkable water. And, as we know, bee populations are nearly wiped out, and attempts to artificially replicate their ecological role have failed. Life expectancy continues its upward climb in the West, with declining tolerance for anyone over the age of ninety-five. We must make our decisions on this issue, and– Excuse me!'

His squealer was ringing. Lifting it to his ear, he said that he had given instructions he was not to be disturbed.

A message was quietly delivered. Tibbett sat staring down at his desk. Then, seeming to pull himself together, he beckoned Barrin closer to the podium. He spoke to him behind a sheltering hand.

'You should inform the audience,' Tibbett said. 'It's my sister but it's your province. This is good news. Let's use it to balance the bad news.'

Barrin protested. The Terrier insisted.

Swivelling the wheelchair, Barrin turned to face the audience. He spoke, with a tremor in his voice.

'I know this family on Tharsis. The partness' name is Sheea. He's Phipp. Sheea has borne a living child. A living child! We rejoice at this news.'

The response of the audience was mixed. Many were simply pleased. A few, better informed, remained sceptical.

Barrin continued.

'Some of you academics may know this but thousands of ordinary people have been kept in ignorance. But I must now state plainly

31

that until this child of Sheea's arrived alive, no woman on Tharsis has ever borne a living child. Baby bodies were born broken, distorted, dead . . .'

He paused to choke back tears. 'Yes, broken, dead, some with no legs, some with eggshell skulls, one of them with no brain at all . . .

'The President has said I should tell you this. So far, only eighty-five babies have been born in the West tower. And all were stillborn.'

There were some aghast cries from the audience at his words.

'Yes, still-born. Eighty-five. Malformed, as I've said. The grief of it . . . impossible to describe.'

A woman in the audience shouted, 'How did this happen? How could it happen?'

Barrin could not go on. Tibbett took over, to continue in a slightly steadier voice. 'The number of these miscarriages has tailed off, these last two years – simply because Tharsis women refuse to become pregnant, knowing, fearing, what the outcome will almost inevitably be.

'Sheea is – we all believe – incredibly fortunate. Her child lives.

'He was born only a couple of hours back. Sadly, he is deformed and is not well. We will keep this information from the public.

'But the great thing is we have a living Martian child at last!'

Most of the audience rose and clapped. Then the questions began. Eighty-five stillbirths! How could it be?

6

Mangalian Among the Ladybirds

A small courtyard behind one of the buildings of the Sorbonne in Paris contained an oak bench and table. The news of the birth had not yet reached Paris. Mangalian, unaware of the momentous news, was sitting relaxing on a bench. He had been guest lecturing to the Earth Sciences students on the colonisation so far, and the merits of going to live in what he had described as 'the new old world' of Mars. After lunch, a debate had been held with Mangalian and Adrien Amboise on one side – for the necessity of the Martian venture – and a group of German and Chinese scientists on the other.

Sunshine bathed the courtyard with mellow light and warmth. In the cracks between the flagstones with which the courtyard was paved, small weeds had sprung up. In one of the cracks near Mangalian grew a little yellow flower with tiny spiked petals and a fuzzy rich heart the size of a baby's fingernail.

Mangalian was idly watching a ladybird. It crawled over the leaves of the weed to the flagstone, where it made haste to walk to the distant stalk of another weed. On reaching the stalk, the insect climbed it, opened its wing case, and flew away.

He wondered what impulse governed it. Could it feel contentment or discontent? On what did it feed? How would it die? He had not studied such matters, although he imagined the insects went from eggs to larvae to the adult form he had been watching. What could it feel like to undergo such a transformation? Would humanity undergo as dramatic a transformation on Mars? What might happen to Rosemary? – Rosemary who had taken flight just like the ladybird.

He realised at that point – as a man was approaching from the nearby building – that his ladybird had no spots on its wing-case. He had assumed that all ladybirds had spots. Possibly this was a new evolutionary variety, adapting to the environs of Paris.

The man approaching stood before Mangalian, smiling. This was Adrien Amboise, Professor of Medical Studies at the Sorbonne. Amboise was about forty-five, trim and sporting a small moustache. He wore a gown. His father had worked at the Max Planck Institute in Germany, where he had fallen in love with and married in old-fashioned style the elegant German woman whose researches led to the later discovery of the normon.

Mangalian admired both Adrien's father and his intellectually formidable mother. And, normally, would delight in conversation with Adrien. However, at the moment, he wanted only an hour's peace, but he rose and the men shook hands. 'I apologise for interrupting your reverie.'

'Don't worry. I was only thinking about ladybirds.'

Amboise looked confused. After a slight pause, he said, 'I too am an admirer of the ladies.'

'What can I do for you? Do you wish to apply to me for a life on Mars?' Mangalian was speaking jokingly, after relaxing in the sun and not feeling avid for conversation. He had been thinking of Rosemary Cavendish, regretting that he had been so chaste where she was concerned. But there had been a kind of hauteur in her manner. Well, all that was but a dream . . . Already, it was five years since Rosemary had left Earth for her Tharsis occupation.

'Sadly, monsieur, the idea of living on Mars is a bad dream, so I have come to believe.' Adrien Amboise endeavoured to show regret. He stood there poised and graceful, in a suit, in the sun, smiling politely as he gazed at Mangalian, who had showed no inclination to get up from his chair. 'I would support you in a debate, but that is not for me. Here on Earth, continual disturbance, distraction, disaster . . . but on Mars – what? Continual boredom . . . And the unresolved stillbirth problem . . .'

'Yet to be on that silent planet, Adrien . . . Isn't that a wonderful success? Applied science . . . It's a dream that has been pondered for some centuries and is now more than just a dream – a waking dream which–'

'Oh, of course for over two centuries there have been stories – as there have been ghost stories – what you may call the science fiction – but they are made for superficial adventure, as the often uninspired writing indicates–'

'Ah, so you are not only a medico but a critic of literature!' Mangalian, with a curl of his lip, stared into the distance as he spoke.

'No, no, no, but such tales had no true deliberation, only conveying thrills of conquest or doom. A shallow fiction . . .'

Mangalian would not let such a sweeping generalisation pass. 'Well, sir, as a mere boy on San Salvador, I happened on a story by a Mr Wells. Later in life, I heard he was celebrated and respected, although he wrote of things that did not exist in reality. This particular book that caught my fancy was called *The War of the Worlds*, although I found it was rather "The War against Woking", of which I had never heard until then. That story denigrates mankind. It is a chastisement, a real fiction, an analogy. There is no hero – or if there is a hero, then it is a bacillus.'

Amboise stared up at the sky, as if in the hope that his impatience might steam off to the troposphere. 'But H.G. Wells was an exception. A chastisement, as you put it. It does not prove the rule. Immediately after Mr Wells's book appeared, an American journalist wrote a sequel in which a fleet of ships led by a Professor Edison went to Mars and knocked – what is your phrase? – yes, knocked hell from them . . . You see, no morality, just violence. The irony of Wells is lost amid all the aggression.'

Mangalian did not answer, merely sighing. Silence fell.

Amboise feared he had offended the visitor.

'I do not object to fantasy, please understand me. Indeed, in my boyhood I read a story called *The Sword of Rhiannon*, set on an imaginary Mars. It was a romance pure and simple, aiming only at a pretty tale. In my memory the simple prose held no subordinate clauses, not one. I am no snob. I loved that story.'

Mangalian became stony-faced. 'Have you another subject in mind to discuss?'

7

The Care of a Child

'Excuse me,' said Amboise. He thrust his hands into his trouser pockets, indicating that he was only partially regretful for his remarks. 'I wished to make the point that any idea of mankind – including the ladies of whom you and I are so fond – actually living on this Planet Rouge is meretricious. Not only will humanity there slowly die out, but there is a more serious aspect.'

'Such as?'

'I may phrase it briefly,' said Amboise. 'You UU people, if I may so call you, m'sieu, have a selection procedure whereby intelligent and balanced personalities are accepted to fly away and be lost to this world – which badly requires them. We need precisely such people here, m'sieu. There is a shortage of the grave and the good.'

A tabby cat jumped off the nearby wall. It sat upright, front paws together, watching the two men as if sitting in judgement upon them.

'I see your point,' said Mangalian, 'but the universities of

Bordeaux and Toulouse evidently do not, since they have already joined the UU.'

Amboise swept away both Bordeaux and Toulouse with a gesture of his hand. 'We require those fine personalities here because we need hope in the world. Such personalities represent a saner future. No more missile systems but systems of civilised living. Such is my hope.'

'Hope? But it is hope that overcomes all difficulties and takes us to Mars. The colony has now been working for – what? Almost ten years. No living child born as yet, malheureusement, but . . . You are hoping against hope because you can see this world of ours, this worn old world, is still without sanity or balance, despite all the wise and well-intentioned personalities there have ever been, of both sexes, over the centuries.'

Amboise sighed. 'Yes, and also those millions who live quiet lives. Who perform minor good works for the unfortunate – the feeding of the infirm, let's say, the reading of stories to illiterates – in their squares and streets and possibly homes. But perhaps they did not disturb themselves with hope and had to live for the day.'

'That's a waste of resources, sir. A vegetable existence. It's better to be pessimistic, to worry about the world, to reach out for a new thing, a new chance, to be never satisfied.' Mangalian paused, remembering. So he had let Rosemary go; she was now but a name. 'I grew up among brothers and sisters. We were happy but mischievous. We regretted we lived confined to such a small island as San Salvador. Excellent swimmers, yes, but poor thinkers. Perhaps that may be what prompts me as an adult to regret we live on such a small planet.'

'. . . and Mars is even smaller,' said Amboise, smiling falsely.

'You'll find that its land area is the equal in extent to Earth's.'

With his hands in his pockets, Amboise strolled about in a circle, thinking, his shadow forming a confused pattern at his feet. The cat moved cautiously away from him. 'We are not getting far, Mr Mangalian. Albert Einstein was quoted as saying, "Learn from yesterday, live for today, hope for tomorrow." My hope is also for tomorrow, that you can retain your useful scheme of UU, but you do not send into exile people who are our "hope for tomorrow".'

Impatiently, Mangalian said, 'There is a conflict of hope. You do not, I believe, hope at all. You fear. If I agree with that quote from what's-his-name, I do truly hope for tomorrow, hope for, strive for, a new and better existence on our neighbouring world.'

Amboise gave a strained laugh. 'As a keen horseman, I have no wish to be ever on Mars. I understand that the planet suffers from permanent grass shortage.'

Mangalian shrugged. 'Maybe, in time, our descendants will discover existences far beyond the modest world of Mars. Human beings will always struggle for greater understanding. We know conditions will be harsh initially, but we shall triumph.'

'Conditions will not be harsh. They will be impossible.'

'You see, you have no hope! In any case, I cannot halt what already has momentum beyond my control. You should voice your fears elsewhere. Come to a UU meeting. I must go. I have another appointment.'

He nodded curtly to the Professor of Medical Studies, rose, and walked out of the courtyard. The cat followed him as far as the gate.

An armed guard, Yat, awaited him outside the premises. He cared for Mangalian as if he were his child.

And Mangalian, when he was a small boy, long before he was big enough to think of chasing women, had certainly loved his father.

San Salvador was not a large island. It grew sugar cane. Mangalian's father had been a sharecropper – cast off by his employers without pension as was the custom at the age of sixty. He walked with the aid of a staff taller than himself, painted white. He walked slowly, so that his son could easily keep up with him.

His father liked to stroll by the sea. They would walk along the front, past the row of thatched-roof shops until they came to the last shop, a small café.

There they sat, under a large sun umbrella. Father would order Coke. Sometimes they would talk. Father liked to spout old country sayings. 'Just because you're an idiot don't mean to say you're sillier than me.' 'You can be ready for anything, but that don't say you ain't good for nothin'.'

Father kept a hold of his staff as they listened to the screeching of the gulls and watched the waves break on the shore.

Mangalian went barefoot into the little saloon to buy a second bottle of Coke. A radio perched on a shelf behind the bar was giving out news in a tinny voice.

'Capitalist astronomers in Tampa, Florida, just now claimed that we've got company. We are in what they call a binary system, with a dwarf star out beyond the Oort Cloud. Meanwhile, "Baby-Face" Morte was captured by police last night, about to set off for Cuba. Charged with the murder of the dancer, Francesca Pagnesa–

Clutching the Coke bottle, Mangalian went out to his father.

'Pop, what's a binary system?'

'Son, that just means there's two of whatever. Fact is, the more you learn, the more you find you don't know.'

The gulls still sailed and screeched overhead, as if in mockery.

His son looked down at the sand between his bare toes. Later, as an adult, Mangalian liked to say that this was the moment when he decided he must get off the island, put on shoes, and start learning about astronomy and many other things with which the capitalist world seemed stocked.

So he liked to say. He could even recall the taste of the Coke. But memory was uncertain – although the anecdote made a good tale when, much later, he was being interviewed at one grand meeting or another.

BABY BOOM ON RED PLANET
NO WATER – BUT CHRISTENING NOW DUE
'A MIRACLE' SAYS MARVELLING MOTHER
IT'S A BOY! EVEN BETTER: IT'S ALIVE

Such were some of the headlines in squealers and squeakers all round the world, driving out the exciting news that nine hundred intending immigrants from Africa had been shot dead within Italian waters, off the coast of Catanzaro.

Other news began to re-emerge, but Mars still appeared in some headlines.

KUWAIT ON FIRE – SEGREGATION RIOTS TO BLAME
ITALIAN PRESIDENT'S PARTNESS POISONED
TWENTY UN TROOPS KILLED IN KALMYTSKAYA
THARSIS CELEBRATES NEW BABY

In fact there was little celebration in the Tharsis settlement, as the Terrier found when he spoke on the shrieker. A small Chinese delegation came to offer felicitations to the Western tower. Phipp officiated at the gate in a suppressed rage. Local people, aware that Sheea had taken another lover and wishing to tease, or not knowing he'd quarrelled with Sheea, kept congratulating him. But the amazing baby had been sired by someone unknown.

Sheea still would not give the name of her lover, and was in a weakened state, needing nursing. Her baby lay by her side. It was of a yellowy colour and malformed. Oxygen was being fed to it through a Perspex mask.

'But how is Dolores herself?' the Terrier asked.

Twenty minutes was consumed in getting word to Mars, with another twenty minutes for a response.

'She is in a somewhat depressed state, but being brave. The child is still alive. But unconscious.' Such was the response from a nurse who then severed communication.

Tibbett found he needed a strong drink.

Daze and Piggy, two of Sheea's three Earth-born children, sat anxiously near their mother's bed, speaking – when they spoke – in whispers. Squirrel, Sheea's senior child, was nowhere to be seen.

As Phipp grudgingly let in the Chinese delegation, one of the men stared curiously at him. Ill-tempered as he was, Phipp challenged the man.

'What are you staring at me for?'

'No, I don't stare,' was the reply. 'You are to be congratulated to have a living child born here. Why you are not pleased?'

For answer, Phipp seized the man by the throat and shook him.

Uproar broke out. Guards burst in. The Chinese punched Phipp.

Phipp was dragged away, kicking savagely. The guards pushed him into a side chamber. 'What the hell are you thinking about, you fool? You have disgraced us. The Chinese are – or were – our friends.'

'Look, some bastick got up my partness. Why not that guy – giving me that gloating stare?'

'You're psychotic. Why should some Chinese guy sneak into her bed? And you don't own Sheea. We don't do such things here. It's psychoanalysis for you. And you've lost your job.'

The news of this incident circulated fast. No one was happier to hear that Phipp would be confined than was his son Squirrel. Still, Squirrel could not bring himself to face his mother. Just a half hour of dear wicked pleasure and he was disgraced for ever – yes, disgraced, even if his act had produced the first living Martian baby . . .

He could never tell anyone about that.

8

The Death of a Hero

Barnard and Lulan escorted Barrin by ambulance to St Thomas's Hospital in the heart of London. He had collapsed just as the session ended. The hospital buildings were surrounded by solid concrete blocks, one storey high. Armed men looked out from the rooftops. Suicide-bombers had attacked the hospital almost from the moment Barrin had arrived, indifferent to any other casualties.

These attackers, the faithful, acted in accord with a passage from the Koran which says, 'Neither on earth nor in heaven shall you escape His reach: nor have you any besides God to protect or help you. Those that disbelieve God's revelations and deny that they will ever meet Him shall despair of My mercy. A woeful punishment awaits them.'

His people's response to a visitor from Mars was 'Kill him!' or 'Burn him!'

Barrin was settled in a ward of his own. Attention was immediately given to his lungs and heart. He lay supported by a breathing apparatus, his legs under local anaesthesia, while undergoing analysis under Earth gravitation. His heart had become too weak to circulate blood under the increased gravity.

'I fear I cannot,' he began to tell the doctor who attended him. He saw but could not focus. She who sat by him was nothing but a shadow. 'Survive,' he managed at last.

'You just need a little repair,' she said, comfortingly. 'You are brave. You have a medal for it. Interplanetary travel is an attack on both body and intellect.'

'Not on intellect, ma'am.' It was his twilight. 'Space exists to be travelled.' His voice died away on the word 'travelled' while he fought for another breath. 'We are, aaaafter all, products of the . . . of th' cosmos.' Had he said what he meant to say? Speech was such an effort. 'Products of th' compass,' he murmured, trying again. He panted.

'Bug–' was all he managed to say. Then '–ger', on a dying fall.

She held his hand, regarding him gravely. 'Are we in some way a dream of the cosmos? Although it goes against my profession, I mean the profession of healing, I sometimes find myself inclining to a belief that we are insubstantial beings.'

He blinked at her, acknowledging that indeed he was a prime example of an insubstantial being.

'After all, religions that do not entail worship of graven images worship insubstantial gods, monstrous creatures that cannot be seen or heard any more than creatures of fiction, creatures supposedly ruling the entire world. The Christian god is an example.

'We may in a sense be insubstantial in such a way as him. We create him in our image and not vice versa, as the Bible claims.'

Barrin sighed. He was not well enough for such irritating banality. He heard his heart thudding in his ears. 'But still–' he began, only to find he could not complete the sentence. He did not even know what the sentence was going to be. 'Still . . .'

The doctor mopped Barrin's forehead with a damp tissue. 'I was always struck by that passage in Plato's *Republic*. About the shadows seen in the cave? I expect you know it.'

In feeble irritation he whispered he had never heard of Plato, in the hope she would cease talking.

She regarded him as a special case, one recognised by the King's medal. To have been to Mars and back earned her respect, yet she felt that behind that compulsion (as she saw it) lurked illusion.

Even as she told him Plato's analogy, Barrin felt himself drifting away.

It was indeed a striking analogy, so striking that it had lived for something like twenty-five centuries. Some people have been imprisoned in a large cave since childhood. They are unable even to move their heads and must always stare in front of them. (Just like us, she said.) Somewhere behind them bright lights shine. Between the bright lights and the prisoners is a raised walk. Free persons pass along this walk. Their shadows are thrown on the cave wall at which the prisoners have no alternative but to stare. Were they to hold a discussion with one another concerning life, they would assume that those shadows before them were the real, the only, things. They would make of them what sense they could.

'So, my dear Barrin, do you not see that truth could prove to be nothing but mere shadows?'

He made no response. She felt for his pulse. There was no pulse.

'Just as I talk to you, my dear, now but a shadow,' she said with sorrow.

Late in the afternoon, when the doctor was off duty, she sat grieving with her partner by the fountain in their garden, attempting a light meal. There were butterflies on the buddleia and a nuthatch in the rhododendron bushes.

She said, 'Barrin was the first, the *only*, person to reach Mars and return here. Oughtn't we to start a fund to raise a statue to him? Better than that medal, which hardly anyone saw . . . You don't seem to grasp how unique his achievement was?'

'Get on with your gazpacho, dear,' her partner said.

Barrin's death took up a lot of air space. Another rival for attention was the invasion and take-over of Greenland by Russo-Musil forces. The world was so full of disturbances that the fate of Greenland seemed unimportant. It was not a particularly popular tourist resort. The leader of the invasion, and now the president of the state, was Colonel Ketel Mybargie, his name sounding quite friendly. He had announced, 'We have taken over Greenland for spiritual purposes. This we trust will benefit all native Greenlanders.'

Most of the world, with troubles of their own, were prepared to be reassured by these words, unaware that native Greenlanders had already been reduced almost to single figures.

9

Life Elsewhere?

The squealers produced varieties of uncomfortable news.

In the Middle East, President Iduita Gane admitted to, indeed boasted of, the desecration of Westminster Abbey, carried out on the grounds that it had become a refuge for gay men. More seriously, the small university in 'Lhasa', Tibet, withdrew from the UU, pleading poverty. Since the university was under direct Chinese control, this move was seen as a first reprisal for the attack on a visitor at the West's tower gate.

A counter move was also reported. The Florida universities, a group calling itself 'Tampa' within the UU, were celebrating the anniversary of their sighting of Earth's companion sun, 'Nemesis'. They offered a peace-making infusion of finance to 'Lhasa'. The offer was 'being considered'.

In small print at the bottom of the flash, it was announced that some of 'the gallant' Barrin's possessions had gone missing.

*   *   *

The Terrier and the Grey Wolf, ignoring the medal, had in fact taken hasty possession of Barrin's rather old-fashioned shrieker. It contained the Terrier's parting advice to Barrin as the latter had prepared for his journey back to Mars. Directed at Barrin, it had been given as an off-the-record talk, with a small audience of trusted colleagues. It had taken place before that routine committee meeting which had turned out to be Barrin's last.

They played the recording to a select few on the UU Council.

Tibbett's talk had begun with an item he thought wiser to keep restricted for the present:

'So far, governments have mainly regarded the UU as something of a derisible exercise, an eccentricity that could not be maintained for long. But, there are also some cautious signs of approval because, during a time of severe recession, the Mars expedition brought employment and a modicum of life to a sluggish economy.

'I have to warn you that opinion in Washington has shifted under the new President. Planners, military men and others are considering bringing UU under government control. Don't you hate planners? Don't you hate military men? We are doing all we can to disabuse them, short of cutting the President's throat . . .

'Remain constantly aware that the UU is not a united body but a series of wise or ambitious or just plain crazy heads of educational establishments. You are not dealing with a church, a united body, although of course we think highly of the UU. The Principals of some universities, pleading poverty, wish to withdraw their support; they claim they gain nothing in the way of knowledge as a return. Some wish to prune their contributions, or to send their subscriptions less frequently.

'A learned if short-sighted man from Stockholm suggested we should turn to governments for a hand-out. While we would appreciate a hand, we are old enough to savvy that some hands have a vice-like grip. You will understand, my dear brave Barrin, that the last thing we want is governmental involvement, which would probably transform our quiet assembly of towers into a military outpost.

'In some cases political motives predominate which have little to do with us. In some cases, the Indonesian universities for example, they entered the union for complex reasons beneficial to themselves, having suffered badly from fault-line disturbances and consequent earthquakes and tsunamis. You might find it expedient to mention this case, stressing that on Mars you do not suffer from fault-lines. Tsunamis too are singularly lacking.'

He smiled but the audience did not find the remark very funny.

'Take what advantages you can out of our situation. In particular, the news that we live in a binary system has caused the population at large to take a new view of our cosmic status. In fact, a change of umwelt.

'You must nevertheless continue to emphasise the rigours of life on Tharsis, and above all how you are now, and shall be for a while, entirely dependent on the UU's many scientific and humane contributions. If you can do that, it would be wise also to stress how you are working towards independence – positive night soil strategies, for example, with potential for growth of potatoes – so that the UU consortium do not convince themselves that their contributions will prove unending.

'Recall too that the towers often send out expeditions over the surface of Mars, in search of previous life forms.'

A pause followed while Barrin gathered himself together.

'How do you advise treating the religious question, should it arise?' Barrin asked from his wheelchair. He looked a sick man, quite unfit to make a journey to the Moon, never mind back to Mars.

The Terrier paused to blow his nose, perhaps to delay answer.

It was an opportunity for a humourist in the audience. 'As we are part of a binary system, will our taxes be doubled?'

Whereupon the Grey Wolf spoke, ignoring the laughter. 'By the lack of comment regarding our quest for previous Martian life forms, I take it you have a scorn, as do many people, for the mere notion of life on Mars. A Professor Lowell in the early years of the Twentieth Century spread the notion of, as he quaintly put it, "Mars as the Abode of Life". The idea then became quite fashionable. "Martians" became a serious subject for conversation. But then the comics got hold of them and for a number of years the concept of two-legged green people became laughable.'

'They're even more laughable now,' Barrin murmured.

'Oh yes,' the Grey Wolf agreed. 'But the idea of life itself is again the subject of serious contemplation.'

The Terrier took over again.

'Your question, Barrin – the belief in life elsewhere resembles a religion. One of the hallmarks of most religions is "life elsewhere". It is bound to recur, along with other metaphysical riddles. Of course the UU know that the colonists are all atheist, or at least agnostic. Remember that a clause about atheism was written into our original charter. It almost provoked a war.

'This was one of the several reasons we were, sadly, unable to introduce Muslims to Mars. Not that there were many Muslim universities willing to contribute. True, there were some Muslim communities that would have been welcome – Malaysia, for instance. Also those dissident Muslims in China in – what's it called? – Urumchi.'

'So if we are accused of excluding a large proportion of the human race, what precisely is the defence, President?' Barrin asked.

'A large proportion excludes itself . . .'

There, in the middle of the Terrier's response, the recording cut out.

Over coffee after that talk, the Grey Wolf had been asked the same question about religion. She had smiled as she began to count on her fingers for emphasis.

'Firstly, the great majority of humanity would hate to go there, fear the journey, fear Mars itself.

'What if we find it proves to be inhabited by non-humans hiding somewhere?' Another finger.

'What if it proves never to be truly habitable, if those of us already there are forced to go back?' A third finger.

'But the ruling in our UU charter states categorically that there is to be no religion on Mars. I was a script girl when the charter was set up, and one of the council's fears was that a new religion might spring up, become indigenous and prove even more of a cause for division than do terrestrial religions.'

In her earnestness, her fingers were forgotten.

A recorder clerk spoke.

'That doesn't quite answer the question about mass exclusions. After all, there are forward-looking people everywhere. Many would be proud to join us.'

'You will have to explain to them how limited are our Martian facilities.'

One of the women from the Exploration Desk laughed. 'Oh, the toilets, you mean? But thousands of Muslims live happily without toilets. And Africans. And—'

'Stop it! Yes, we did have an initial problem without plentiful water. But that's been solved the Chinese way, with night soil distribution and so forth. Do not let yourself be drawn into such minor arguments. Just remember the ghastly complexities of terrestrial global wars and the unrest we experience everywhere.

'For the majority of inhabitants, oppression, shortages, racism, tribalism, sexism, rapine, and of course the kaleidoscope of religions, makes existence a living hell.'

'It's the old lungs and penises problem,' a man remarked.

The Grey Wolf, undeflected, said, 'Such issues interest only the washed and well-dressed and wily. If you want to assist, you must get what you can from them. Neither beg nor boast. See if they are researching a quicker way to get supplies out to Tharsis.'

As the group shook hands and put cheek to cheek, the Grey Wolf had pressed her lean cheek to the Terrier's whiskery one.

Those who lived in the towers took exercise. Tennis was popular. Sport itself did not entirely exercise their minds. But they feel themselves to be closer to the mystery. The mystery was alluring, even obsessional. Nor was it easy to define. But there certainly was a mystery.

'Life is the invisible elephant in the room,' as someone put it.

The mystery lodges in the skulls of humans.

See, here's a man. It's night and he sits by a small fire in a forest. The seasons are turning; it grows colder. His woman lies by his side, not asleep but with no speech or movement. The man has a dog, part wolf, on a leash, made restless by the crackle of burning sticks.

These three beings are in a continent almost uninhabited. It is full of trees. The trees grow straight, in silent competition, one with another. The man tears branches off the trees to burn, to keep him warm. He sits there, hands out to the blaze.

He thinks. He is attempting to think about the mystery.
He can't even name it, but he feels its presence.

Enormous lengths of time, lengths beyond human visualisation, stand
between the present and that moment when the universe exploded
from a nothingness – nothingness also beyond human visualisation.
The illuminations of that distant beginning have sunk into almost
complete night. Fires burn out.

Yet the dust and debris of that beginning still continue to fly outwards.
The universe, to use a phrase we almost understand, continues to
expand. We label some of the clusters of blazing material galaxies. Stars
are lit in these galaxies, yet throw no light on their meaning.

Suppose there is no meaning in a galaxy and we are just wasting
our time. No meaning in a galaxy – or in the whole universe? Why
should there be? The strange thing is that human entities who worry
about this question exist. It may be that mind lends meaning. Is that
what mind is for? We have to live, to die; neither is a voluntary
process. Yet we find what happens between birth and death important,
to have meaning.

The wily squirrel, clearly a conscious being, prefers its tree. But
we have come down from the trees to face – or to invent – the mystery
alone.

So human life, let us say for a moment, has meaning. Does that
mean also that the existence of viruses holds a meaning for them?
Animals certainly have minds. But no concept of Mind.

These days, we can departmentalise this mystery into scientific,
religious and philosophical slots – even if we believe that all three
departments form one invisible elephant in our thinking.

And another elephant. The telescope at Tampa had actually
managed to pinpoint Nemesis, the Massive Solar Companion – in
fact a dull dwarf star. It proved that Earth had been a component
in a binary system, without an inkling of the fact, throughout all
history and prehistory.

And if there is no understanding, then what meaning can there
be in human life? Or supposing the universe has a meaning –
supposing it is its own meaning – does that give human life meaning?
And what if 'meaning' itself holds no meaning?

Here we ask questions which are sometimes put less naively round the desks and tables in the settlement, in the evening relaxation period, except in Singa-Thai, where they dance.

We hope the questions probe the mystery more clearly than does the man squatting by his fire in the great forest of the night on that forbidding continent. But do they get closer to answers?

A mathematician, by name Daark, works on Noel's computer. His character has changed since his life on Earth. He had a partness and two children, but his career was failing. On Tharsis, a measure of remorse makes him a solitary in the crowd. It was he who had built on Madame Amboise's work, and discovered the normon. He drew up an equation which proved that the universe itself is a life form.

This solution proved unwelcome. There are now other clever people who are seeking to disprove Daark's proof.

One man, Nors, committed suicide in order to prove that if Daark's figures were correct and the universe itself was a life form, then suicide would be impossible.

10

The Inevitable Happens

Grey Wolf and Terrier were at home in their Harpstead house when news came through on the squeaker. 'Hello. We greatly grieve to have to tell you sad news. Regrettably, the Sheea baby has died, age just seven days. It had been suffering from multiple internal injuries. The mother is well, but naturally upset, as are all here. We are now seeking advice from gynaecologists in terrestrial clinics.'

'Oh, Dolores! Dearest Dolores!' cried the Terrier, reverting to his sister's childhood name when he heard the news.

'I feared this would happen,' said Grey Wolf as she wrapped herself round her partner and let him weep his burning tears. 'All the poor little Mars babies die.'

Noel had been present, consoling Sheea, when three doctors – all the tower could muster – had taken her dead baby to a nearby examination chamber. It resembled a small plucked, uncooked turkey. Dr Gior had been with the midwife when the child was delivered.

'It was living when it emerged, although the ribs were not properly formed. There was a pulse, but no breathing.' Noel's eyes filled with tears as the doctor spoke.

'As you will know,' said Dr Cood, folding his hands before him on the table, 'the heart can continue to beat even when the brain has ceased to function. At least for a while. I attached the mechanical ventilator – the heart muscle operates on its own. Unfortunately, it was at that point the midwife went off, all excitement, and announced that the child was living. We failed to correct her misapprehension immediately. We kept the baby on the ventilator for a week, but it was already brain dead. And so, unfortunately, the world was misled.'

Dr Nivec agreed. 'It's that vital lowest part of the brain where it merges with the spinal cord. The union there broke just before or during the actual birth. So brain death took place immediately, although the lungs continued to operate after a fashion . . . What can we do about this dire situation?'

Dr Cood sighed heavily. 'You may remember some idiot at the Sorbonne – was his name Adrien Amboise? – suggested that when a woman here found herself pregnant she should be flown back to a terrestrial maternity home. Even if the flight could be made short enough, the rigours of it would most probably kill both her and the foetus!'

'Absurd!' said Gior.

'Ridiculous!' said Nivec.

'Typical of Earth people!' agreed Cood.

Noel laughed briefly. She told them the compoutat was recording. She reproved them for talking in generalities. Hard facts were necessary.

Dr Gior spoke, saying that the human gestation period was normally 40 weeks. A child born before the thirty-seventh week is defined as premature on Earth. Here, on Tharsis, women give birth at thirty-six weeks, with few exceptions.

She said they were working on a theory that the problem was not only one of the lighter Martian gravity, serious though that was. The rigors of the Terra-Mars journey caused a lowering of temperature of a woman's womb. That and the irregularity of breathing had a lasting effect. A bacterium mycoplasma was also under suspicion. Antibiotics had been used to delay labour, but had now been shelved. Part of the problem of treatment was that they had insufficient equipment.

Drugs called tocolytics were used which caused only a slight retarding of delivery. They were believed to allow a little time for steroids to strengthen the baby's lungs and bones. Sheea had been given this treatment, but . . .

At this point Gior spread her hands in a gesture of despair.

Dr Cood mopped his bald head, saying, 'We're still at work on the whole question. It was totally unforeseen. It is the most serious problem we face.'

Nivec added, muttering, 'If the problem remains unsolved, then the very existence of our colony on Mars is brought into question, obviously. It is probable to my mind that the UU may withdraw their funding.'

'And then?' Noel asked.

It was Nivec who replied. 'We'll have to think of something.'

11

A Belated Announcement

At 6:30 was the daily Brightener, the meeting of experts, informal, information being passed on. Speculation. Jokes, even.

'Why are Martians so light-hearted?'

'Because on Earth they have weightier matters.'

'Why are Martian men not so light-hearted?'

'Because as Martian dwellers they have lighter members.'

General chat spread round the table. Aymee was first to call for general attention.

'It's really not my field, if we can claim to have fields on Tharsis, but I was thinking about the used supply rockets, just lying around. Wasted! Since we are stretched for finances, why can't we launch them back empty into a Lunar orbit, to be overhauled and used again?'

'We don't have any launchers this end, Aymee.' So said Troed, the deep-voiced chief engineer.

'Can't we build one with assistance from the other settlements?'

'You might have something there, Aymee,' said Daark. Aymee fluttered her eyelids at him, expressing gratitude for his support. 'After initial costs –' He was punching his watputer – 'Building a launcher and so forth . . . yes, UU could reclaim the supply rockets lying idle for reuse. Save over 7.5 million per flight . . .'

'So then we'd maybe get better quality food stocks.' So said Daark, without the need for further computation. Aymee smiled with delight at her cleverness.

That comment sent smiles all around the table, until the dark-haired slender Noel, immaculate as usual – often known behind her back as 'Know-All' – raised her hand to speak. Noel was cousin to the Barrin now a guest of the UU on Earth. She hadn't shared her knowledge that, from the medical reports, it was likely that Barrin was dying even as she spoke.

She said she wished to engage the group in a discussion of the childbirth crisis on Tharsis.

Immediate silence fell. Everyone knew that this was a serious subject, more pressing, more distressing, than the used rocket cases.

'You will all know someone who has carried a child, only to have it die at or just before birth. We're all busy here, occupied with so many things. Perhaps you have not registered the fact that no living child has yet been born in our tower. Not to live, without full life-support, for more than a few minutes . . .'

She repeated her phrase. 'No living child,' tapping the table with her forefinger for emphasis.

'This is the most tragic matter we could possibly face.

'All children have either been stillborn or have been on their last gasp as they emerge from the womb, dying within four minutes, or in one exceptional case fifteen minutes. The life of Sheea's baby was prolonged artificially. It was no more healthy than the others. Eighty-six of our progeny have died.'

'Don't you think we'll adapt? We've adapted in other ways already – breathing is far easier than when I first arrived.' Daark looked concerned as he spoke, as if not believing his express optimism.

'You think we should just hang around and everything will be okay? Women may be too old to conceive by then . . .'

Something like a united groan went round the table.

'Surely you've got the numbers wrong, Noel?'

'That can't be right? What does the midwife say?'

'Is it the doctor's fault?'

'The midwife's?'

'The father's?'

'Or the mother's?'

'It *must* be something the mother's done wrong . . .'

'I don't believe it,' said one of the astronomers in a hushed tone that indicated he did not want to believe it.

A woman took him up sharply. 'Whatever you care to think, I'll tell you different. My little boy died only a week before he was due. It's a terrible grief, almost unbearable . . .'

Comments rattled round the room. Everyone was dismayed. The knowledge of so many stillbirths had been suppressed, even within the local wards. The images of Mars as a pure place, as a great desert not too far from holiness, had now been corrupted by a vision of desiccating corpses scattered like dead snail shells.

Lock and Ooma were on their way to the dormitory, agreeing that they must cooperate more closely with the other towers, when they came across Thirn, weeping childlike in a corner.

'What is it?' Ooma asked. 'Are you pregnant?'

'No man here will have me. I'm too – I'm too shy for casual sex.' Thirn set up a wail. 'I wish I was back on Earth . . .'

'Nonsense, lass,' said Lock, who had been born in Estonia. 'You're safe here. War on Earth is continuous. It rumbles from one area to another, like a thunderstorm.'

'I hadn't thought of it like that,' said Thirn, sniffing. 'So, what?'

'Have you ever thought of anything?' The pair of them moved on.

12
Mulling Over Required

Months passed, with little change. Stocks of food, supplies of many medicaments, were getting low. But the report from Astronomy Local was that the great ship *Confu* was now just about ready for launch from its lunar orbit. Ready and waiting for its next journey to the Red Planet.

If that was a reason for hope, it was also a reason for anxiety.

The irrational had begun to pop up at the morning Brighteners. A woman known as Vooky suggested that since there was such a high preponderance of women on Tharsis, a language should be introduced used solely by women. And if literature would be needed, she would herself be prepared to translate Samuel Johnson's great novel, *The History of Rasselas, Prince of Abissinia.*

A hubbub of agreement and dissent broke out. It was killed by a woman rising to say there had been such a language, called Nushu, flourishing mainly in the Chinese province of Hunan. It had been used for centuries but had died out. Nushu had come into being because of the oppression of women.

A voice from the floor from a woman known as Iggog, said, '"Nushu"? Totally irrelevant! A fragment from a different umwelt! Here we are, endeavouring to live in a new umwelt trying to deal with a dire foetal disaster. If we fail, this entire enterprise also becomes stillborn.'

Ooma agreed. 'Is the jinx with the foetus, or with the mother? Do we know that yet? Does the journey to Mars seriously permanently affect our circulation and heart action? We don't even know that much.' A gloomy silence fell.

Iggog was a small woman of uncertain age. She had a curt manner and was prone to malicious gossip, but was unexpectedly gentle with the women who came anxiously to ask about that ever-discussed question of stillbirths.

'There may be no cure, darlings. Remember what complex creatures you are. Somewhere along the rocky road of evolution, humans collected friendly bacteria which have become symbiotic with us, and live in our, pardon me, guts. Even those of you more diminutive than I' – she permitted herself a twinkle – 'are fully equipped with them. But they may prove to be slow to change, thus upsetting our entire reproductive systems.'

'How long will that take?' one woman asked.

'There's trillions of bifidobacteria – though I've never counted them – in the prettiest female gut. They keep us going, but where they will go themselves we can't tell. Nor can they. I'm sure it's just that the long voyage here has upset them.'

If you include bacteria, more genetic information is stored in the gut, male or female, than in the human genome. The importance of deoxyribonucleic acid, or DNA, is another question discussed among worried females. This long molecular strand could well have been an instruction hastily scribbled down on a human cell by some demigod or other (although there is no holy scripture which happens to have mentioned it), but the inscription seems to have worked fairly well and is copied and transmitted from generation to generation.

Here again come those enchanting, enchaining questions. Supposing the DNA had been a little different? Why is it what it is?

We assume it is essential for the continuity of life. Yet among all the debris flying about in space, we find traces of an amino acid known as glycine, scattering like a light shower of rain on the planets of the solar system.

Glycine is a basic component of proteins without which our kinds of life could not exist.

Supposing the glycine shower falls everywhere . . . then the distant galaxies might well be thronging with life. Perhaps the camp fires burn more brightly in Andromeda, individual existences are longer, calmer, intellects sharper. A slant on eugenics of which we are never likely to have confirmation.

'Message in last night. The Russos from Greenland have occupied Newfoundland.'

'Really? What on Earth for? Is it important?'

'I suppose it would be if you were a Newfoundlander.'

The human brain has its limitations. A resolution of the great eugenic mystery may not be possible. Questions lie in wait for answers. The trap is baited. There was a hope that some approach to some answers might be found on the arid shores of the planet Mars.

Meanwhile, humanity must mull over the discovery of our binary sun, with its orbit about the old sun of 1.5 light years. Many suns are binary; it is not understood why. Humanity has lived happily – or indeed miserably – for centuries without knowing it lived in a binary system. Do similar large revelations await?

It was because the brain has its limitations that there was no one entirely in command of the West tower. Indecision triumphing, Noel – to use her compname – was officially known as Director and Advisor. The compoutat had ears in every chamber in the tower, as well as its range of shriekers and squealers. Such was the pressure on housing that Noel had her bunk moved into the compoutat room. She was frequently the one who heard the news first, which naturally gave her a stronger say in things.

As it happened, Noel was an uncommunicative woman. She had grown up in a home for orphaned girls. She had always felt herself alone in an over-crowded world. While still immature, she allied herself with a man she had just met. She had not loved him, but was prepared to be an attentive partness. She found him violent and sexually overpowering – a brute who used his fists. She began working for Mangalian, who was gentle and liked to please women. She had won Mangalian's attention, and under his influence had become dedicated to the UU project. She studied hard and finally passed all the requisite tests for Martian exile, escaping from her unpleasant alliance.

On Mars she had the company of others, many of whom, like her, had suffered isolation in early youth, and in consequence had adapted to the chills of solitude. She was enthralled by Mars – or rather, more accurately, enthralled by the fact that she was living on this mysterious planet. Her guarded nature responded to the isolation of the Tharsis bulge.

Currently, she had to cope with a spread of depression in the West tower, brought about by the failure of children, emerging from the womb, to live. Dying. Flawed fatally, bringers only of grief.

These gynaecological fatalities had been the one great disaster no one had foreseen.

13
Some False Dispositions

The compoutat had just whispered in its lower mode of many people reduced to doing little but sit about and grieve for the deaths of so many babies. 'I observe in particular the earth-born youth named Squirrel. He seeks out isolated corners. My reading is that he is in an extreme of sorrow or possibly guilt, and may be contemplating suicide. I would advise that someone should contact him. He is at present on your floor beside Closet Six.'

'Thanks, Comp.' Noel decided to go to Squirrel herself. Before she could reach the door, someone buzzed from outside. She opened the door.

There stood a youth brimming with excitement, smacking left palm with right fist. She recognised it was Squirrel, although not from Comp's gloomy description. She exclaimed in surprise.

'I want to speak to the compoutat; can I? I've just this moment had a brill idea.'

'You know we can't have pets, Squirrel. Laws against them. Not enough to feed them on.'

'No, it's not pets. Something heaps more slick than that.'

Of course Noel gave him access. He started off at once, declaring that what was needed was a kind of centrifuge or roundabout. Pregnant women could be whirled round in it for, say, two hours every day. Artificial gravity would be created, enough to set the foetus to building a stronger heart and bones.

'Two hours, Squirrel! Wouldn't that make one terribly sick?'

'You'd do an hour in the morning and an hour in the afternoon.'

'Well. Let's go down and discuss your idea with the chief engineer. We'll see what he says.'

Troed, chief engineer, listened to Squirrel, lips pursed, not saying a word. Finally, he declared that the centrifuge might be a workable proposition. 'We'll simulate it in the compoutat and see what it figures. Don't be too hopeful, lad.'

He called Squirrel two hours later. 'We can make a prototype, okay. Problem is it will gobble up a lot of our electricity reserves. Take my advice, don't boast about this idea. Don't even talk about it, lad. If it gobbles up too much juice, the whole thing's off.'

A day's schedule began with the Brightener. All those not on urgent duty gathered for a morning's discussion of how things were going. The Brightener was intended to chase away any feelings of loneliness or despair. Defying the dire news of continual baby deaths, the objective was to be cheerful and positive, and to talk about future options; tales about how hard life had been on Earth were also welcome.

Those who had some current troubles preferably stowed them away and showed the brighter side of their personalities. A false disposition, it was found, could be zipped on like an overall; some women never took it off. And yet the problem of depression often worked its way into the talk, serpent-like, unobserved until it struck.

They could take their turn on Gerint's next expedition. Gerint was the man in charge of arranging monthly explorations of Martian territory. He was currently organising the next one; yet there were still some who feared the airless emptiness of the outside world.

People clung to their offices in preference to the barrens comprising the Tharsis bulge and beyond.

A middle-aged woman called Thirn, who ran a small stall on the ground floor in which UU tokens could be exchanged, spoke up. 'Back when I was young, I used to have a stall on the sea front. I sold everything – spades, buckets, sticks of rock. Everything. It was fun. My brother helped. The holiday-makers could scarcely drag their kiddies away . . .

'I was a shy little thing then. Still am.' She giggled. 'I had a boyfriend once. He was called Terry Willington. I let him make love to me once at the back of the shop . . . It was over so quickly. I don't think he loved me.'

Weekly UU councils were held on Earth, and in some respects these were similar to the Brightener on Mars. One of the topics on this particular day began with a medical discussion. Bringing up what felt like almost irrelevant history, the unexpected deaths from dermatomyositis of Simpson and Prestwick, over a decade before, were discussed. No fully satisfactory explanation had ever been reached. The illness had attacked heart and lungs and destroyed the men on the trip back from Mars. The earlier hypothesis was that they had been carrying the virus of the disease with them on the expedition. In hindsight, it was almost certainly just the cumulative stress of the journey.

Although the lives of Simpson and Prestwick were well over, their presence lingered as part of history. Their old truck stood unrusting on the shield as their memorial.

14

The Mad Horse &
Ooma's Sad Poem

Adrien Amboise had always avoided taking part in any speculation about that early calamity. He had accepted a role with the gloomy title of Director of Selections; his duty was to see that only those with learned and balanced dispositions qualified for habitation in the new Martian settlement. The death of the two men did not interest him. Their work had been prior to his appointment, their employment only temporary. His interest lay elsewhere.

Amboise was a keen rider, with Dark Rider, a horse of his own. He and a friend, the Catholic Bishop Claude Metaillié, had been taking a break from the pressures of work, riding together high on the Massif Central. There the wind blew warmly and little habitation distracted them. Sometimes they said almost nothing to each other; conversation broke out only over the meal and the wine they shared in one little auberge or another. The subject then generally concerned the presence of God, in which the bishop believed and Amboise did not.

It was with a determination to speak on that very subject that Amboise entered the terrestrial hall that morning.

The medical discussion closed, a short break was taken, after which the Director of Selections was announced.

He began without preamble. 'Two nights ago, I was staying with a friend in a hamlet called Le Dous. There's a moderately comfortable auberge with stabling for horses. We had ridden there on our horses and had seen them properly settled in before we showered and dined.

'I was awakened in the small hours of the night by a knocking noise I identified as a horse kicking at his wooden stall – the stables were in part beneath our bedroom. The noise continued intermittently.

'I took my torch and went down to see what was troubling Dark Rider, my horse.'

'Excuse me, sir, but what has this to do with the matter of selection?' a young woman on the board asked.

'A great deal, as you shall shortly hear.'

Amboise went on to describe how he had turned left at the bottom of the stairs. A little tiled stub of passage led to the stable door. As he laid his hand on the door, a strange feeling of anticipation overwhelmed him, a feeling of exhilaration and extreme fear. Both emotions seemed to clash together like cymbals as he pushed open the door to see the stallion standing there on its hind legs, its front hooves waving, its dark eyes gleaming in darkness, foam and froth dripping from its open jaws. As some of that expelled liquid splashed across Amboise's cheek and neck, he dropped his torch in shock. It shone feebly across sodden cobbles, stamping hooves.

He could only speak the name of his horse.

It roared an answer. 'I am come to you.'

There was a rail for Amboise to cling to while asking weakly, 'Who are you?'

'Wickedness is in many bodies. Intelligence is an ally of wickedness. Wickedness grows like a green ear of wheat!' The great roar of voice rose to the equivalent of an equine shout, so that Amboise shrank back against the wall.

'Wickedness proliferates. Wickedness is spread by intelligence. Nor is all innocence free from wickedness. Is there not a book which tells mankind that it has dominance over all other creatures? Do we not suffer from such wickedness, do we not bleed and die?'

Struggling against that terrible roar, Amboise said, 'Have I not loved you and fed you and cared for you?'

'None of those things. You have only used me and abused my nature for your own gratification.'

The torch was trampled on and dimmed and failed. Only a slender glimmer of moonlight entered the stable, revealing a haunch here, a tossing mane there, a spark elsewhere, darkness overwhelming everywhere.

Tossing its head this way and that, Dark Rider now spoke shudderingly in a quiet voice, saying that mankind had dreamed of and created hell. 'There is no hell, no heaven. Not even in this stable where I am imprisoned. Those things exist only in the mind of man.'

It seemed to the human trembling there that those words 'the mind of man' echoed on and on, even as that the splinter of moonlight lessened.

That great maned head came down to prod his chest. It declared that now mankind had discovered another hell it could occupy. That it was taking great pains to exile there people who would live only in discomfort, creating, spreading, new wickedness.

At a signal from the chairman, the police guard came and took a hold of Amboise's right arm.

'You are sick, sir, and we shall get you swiftly to the hospital. Do not struggle – no harm will come to you.'

Amboise did struggle. As he struggled, he screamed that he must say what he must say. That the great animal had spoken – spoken with the voice of God.

He believed that there in the stinking dark, in the stench of hay and harness and urine, he had heard the voice of God.

The Almighty declared he was not mighty. As his son had been crucified, so he too had power only in the hands and minds of men. And now he was confronted by a new scientific wickedness in that Amboise, Director of Selections, had accepted the rule that no holy persons or those who believed in salvation, or those who struggled against evil for good, or those who endeavoured to be kind, those who did not flog horses or their own kind, those who dressed penitentially and witnessed the wickedness in themselves – all these were confined to what had been once a green globe that was now like a condemned house, on fire and burning fast.

All this was within the compass of Amboise's command. God himself was perishing in the blaze.

'Wickedness! My wickedness! I heard it from my horse's mouth. I wish to resign, I will resign. I will live no more in this position of advantage I have striven for –'

They were dragging him away, three men assisting the police guard, the chairman phoning the mental hospital to alert them to the incoming patient.

Then they all sat there, looking down at the delicately carved wood of the table, not speaking.

'The poor man is insane,' one of the women councillors said at last.

No one there would even venture an opinion.

Only after a long silence did the chairman say, as if it solved everything, 'I have been informed that the horse involved will be shot in the morning.'

The sitting broke up and the members of the committee went into the lounge to discuss Amboise's bizarre outburst.

Albrik Li of Sichuan Sanctuary University spoke. 'The Director of Selections suffered an hallucination. God, even if he exists, does not speak through the voice of a horse.'

But a man from a department of the Tamil Restitution University disagreed. 'We Hindus respect Ganesh, patron of learning . . . Ganesh the elephant, son of Shiva and Parvati, with one broken tusk . . .

'We also venerate our monkey god, so why not a horse?'

Albrik Li stuck his nose in the air. 'Oh, but these are fairy tales, not to be taken seriously . . .' He added, 'I do not go to church. All the same, I love nature.'

'We don't really care at all about nature,' said Judy Bellenger, Inspector of Colleges. 'Otherwise we would not have ruined it. As for religious feeling, that also we have ruined. Religion has now become involved with patriotism – a refuge of scoundrels, as I believe

Samuel Johnson said . . . God – the Christian God – has become something of a refugee. Is he returning?'

She was bored by her own question, knowing it to be unanswerable. She propped her chin on her hand and stared out of the window. A number of people down there were marching along with banners, disrupting the traffic. She could read the words on the banners: 'Ban the Bombshell Surrock'. Cops stood on the sidewalk, unmoving, weapons at the ready . . . She thought, *What does it matter if God is returning or has left for good? The wretchedness of people always remains.* She thought of the pain in her left side.

'Never mind the bloody theology,' she said. 'The question is: What we do about our colleague Amboise and his talking horse?'

'Or what we do about ourselves,' said a wag from Innsbruck Research, setting down his coffee cup.

'Or about God,' said Judy Bellenger. 'We don't want Him on Mars. They have trouble enough.'

At the Brightener on Mars, some disquiet was also in evidence.

Ooma spoke. Her dark unkempt hair straggled over her neck and face as if she were a drowned mermaid.

She said, in her low husky voice, 'We exiles are forced into a situation of unreality. The Brightener hour only imprints falsity upon us.

'Thirn, you talk about your seaside stall as if it were a little paradise. Excuse me, but I cannot believe it. Did not your customers ever force their kids howling from the shop? And were you content in yourself, still there, selling trashy goods, shutting up late in summer? A narrow life, surely? With the great grey sea on your doorstep.'

Noel asked Ooma what point she was making.

'I'm not attacking Thirn. But to my thought, our situation is a pretty dismal one. Why should the human race talk so much about happiness and advancement? Why? Because they are things we can't have. Sadness and loss are things we can have. We should accept them as our lot. Then possibly life would be – well, scepticism and stoicism are great qualities, of far more worth than pretence.'

Thirn said, 'What makes you such an authority on life? I liked my little shop, whatever you may say. And my brother. And my boyfriend.'

'Oh, him again! Was that the only guy you ever had?'

'I wish I hadn't told you about him.' Thirn sounded close to tears.

Ignoring her remark, Ooma said, 'I was originally of Swedish stock. At least, my great grandfather was Swedish, or part-Swede. He was known as a womaniser, but also as a poet. Many of his poems deal with life as full of confusion and human wretchedness, and were widely appreciated – for their truth as well as for their rhyme-schemes. Wretchedness was respected in those days. And as for yourself, you suffered and died young.

'Sven Langkrist – that was my great-grandfather's name – Sven won an award from a society then held in high esteem, the Soldiers of Anomie and the Acidulant, who scorned verse about flowers or landscape, or happy things in general.

'He travelled widely, eventually to marry an English prostitute – a good woman, the family always said – and wherever he went Sven found people much the same: people whose lot was not particularly fortunate and who got by in life as best they could.

'If you will permit me, I will read you his prize-winning poem. It's dated now, but it does express an anomie which, to my mind, we tend to suppress these days – to our detriment. I shall play you a recording I made on my screamer before leaving Earth. The poem seems to be set in the East, which Sven loved. Maybe in Kuala Lumpur.'

Ooma switched on a recording.

> The avenue yields up its fumes by starlight,
> Unpeeling filthy wrappings layer by layer.
> No sleep but harbours something of tomorrow.
> No time-checks, please, and not an uttered prayer.
>
> Be circumspect! Your smiling next-door neighbours
> Prise up your floorboards when the night bat flies.
> Hold tight your genitals in sleep. Meanwhile,
> Moonlight stains the shutters of closed eyes.
>
> And those who come like lovers in their saris
> To imitate the antics of the past
> Will fill their lanes with anybody's banners:
> Repentance dies. Dawn waits. Her breath comes fast.

At least the whores are better dressed this year:
Though we perforce are always on the thrust,
Ripping the fabrics from their tender yonis
In quest of deeper landscapes, charged with lust.

The prick of pleasure functions like a piston
Where action merely generates distaste –
Orgasm, payment: can they cancel out
One moment in annihilation's waste?

Is feeling then a gateway to disaster
Or is it sense that signals us to doom?
While sex, that carnivore, eats what it jousts with,
The ape invades the drawing room.

Delight is scarcely longer than a letter;
Disgust's a library. And yet, and yet –
All Shakespeare's plays paint folly,
To flesh the stage on which our acts are set.

Impatience follows swiftly on our play.
Pay up, and face the suckling light alone!
What have we got, replacing scented night?
Email, false front, memos, the phone . . .

Our modern man with modern fears complete
Must face the life of lust with armoured eye.
The torrid brothel world holds symbols:
Condoms and foreskins hanging out to dry.

'Seven days shalt thou labour'
To fight thy way through purgatory
Not understanding, hoping, coping
With your own immodest story.

A beggar woman crouches on a stone
While passers-by unheeding go their ways.

Her company, a mangy mongrel
For the hideous evening of her days.

This city once knew dawns of livid splendour.
Pollution now rags out the sky in grey.
Do men who rise and shower and drive to office
Know how their lives have been processed away?

For those of us who sleep in nature's doorways
And close our pockets to society's bills
The stones are cheeks whereon we rest our temples –
Meanwhile, the city crawls towards the hills.

Some ghosts may through night's banyan thickets filter,
But waking finds a world still upside down.
By chance, the map we rescued from the gutters
Proved street plan to another unknown town.

This ranked array of shops and tawdry theatres
Drugs us with fantasies. Say, in that bank
Are there not squads of dusky mistresses
Who have the white man still to thank?

I heard a footfall in the smallest hour.
When starting up I thought I saw your face.
But to my challenge came the wistful answer:
'I'm here, but you are in another place.'

Once I was true and you my pure delight,
Your flesh and spirit played my tender host.
But then – your arms were closed to me for ever.
I'm rudderless while you are but a ghost.

Although faint hope may serve as sail and anchor
The sea is hourly storming up the strand.
The candle gutters in a lifeless window.
Missing your heart, I still seek for your hand.

Spectres that through our mazes find their way
Have little coin but circumstance:
On waking we remember only music,
Bare thigh, dark hair, that look askance.

Newborn, the sun at mosque and supermart
Proclaims that day's the flower of midnight's seed.
The Muslims pray. The rest of us rise up
To face once more the tasks of human need.

'Life's not like that here,' said Iggog, turning up her nose.

'More's the pity,' said Gerint. 'Short of oxygen, short of reality . . .'

'Typical bit of Scandinavian misery,' Iggog responded.

Offended, Ooma said, 'I'd say simply – honest. You can't see Wordsworth or any British writer writing so strongly of a lost life.'

Waiting afterwards for the elevator, Iggog said, 'The guy who wrote that poem – taking advantage of women as per usual . . .'

'No,' said Daark in response. 'He was keeping them in business. Else they might have starved. Look, I think you have a bit of a chip on your shoulder – if you actually think about it, the poet is in pain, condemning himself.'

Iggog contemplated Daark from under her thick brows. 'We'll have a chat about this some time.' Daark inclined his head; he had discovered the normon. He could cope with anything.

On the whole, most people were annoyed that they had been forced to listen to Ooma's poem.

Poetry was one item which had not reached Mars. That river *had* run dry.

15
An Hour's Friendship

Gerint was a silent man usually, of middle age, much of whose time was spent drawing and redrawing maps of the local terrain. He had recently taken to growing a beard, confining it to chin alone.

Gerint would have liked to look more Russian. He had a friend in the Russ-East tower whom he visited on various occasions.

The Russians organised their Martian exile independently. From the beginning they had rejected the idea of reducing their names to cyphers. They used their computers to control comfortable conditions within the tower. They had a small library, at least a couple of shelves, of books – mainly of Leo Tolstoy's novels – in their old physical guise. They also had a studio in which etchings and engravings and some pastels were being created. Some of these works could be exchanged for UU tokens with other towers.

Because of this exchange, Gerint had met with the librarian. They had immediately found interests in common.

Gerint's friend served as librarian and researcher into Russian history. His name was Vladimir Gopman. He showed Gerint a brilliant book on 'The Hermitage' in St Petersburg. The Hermitage contained over three million works of art and artefacts. The two men pored over this beautiful work together.

'Very strong on Matisse,' Vladimir commented.

'Yes. But I don't see any Gauguin, and I remember a wonderful room in the Hermitage full of Gauguins. The Picassos are amazing. His *Woman with a Fan* is extraordinary, don't you think?'

Gerint agreed. 'And a superb Caravaggio . . .'

'Frankly, I am homesick for such beauty,' said Vladimir. 'Can such glory ever occur again? And now Russia has broken up into four states.'

'Many of these artists who depicted such wealth and elegance so brilliantly were poor. Here on Tharsis we have institutional poverty, yet such art can never emerge without the real thing. All this is something I deeply miss.'

'This is why we have become friends,' said Vladimir. 'It is having something in common. But we had to come to Mars to meet that something.'

This suggested a greater kind of intimacy to Gerint than he could easily manage.

'Let me ask you, Vladimir. Time's short. I suppose you are conversant with that splendid tone poem of Borodin's, 'In the Steppes of Central Asia'? It might have been composed with Mars in mind!'

Vladimir shook his shaggy head. 'I've never heard of it. Perhaps Borodin offended someone. But most men here care nothing for works of art.'

Gerint nodded. 'In our tower it's the same. Many important questions engage us. Questions of personality and reality. Of inwardness. But art? A complete blank . . .

'A woman tried a poem on us. Not at all popular . . . Of course, it probably wasn't a very good poem. But I . . . I liked it . . . Well, in two days' time I am taking an expedition out over Tharsis, but somehow I doubt we shall discover any Hermitages.'

'We are not allowed expeditions in case we escape!' They both chuckled.

'To be exiled from exile is really something.'

A warden entered the room. 'Sorry, men. Time's up.'

They had been allowed half an hour's Visiting Time.

As Gerint trudged back to the West tower, he muttered to himself, as if Vladimir were present, 'I'm a renegade. Ardent heathen and lecher that I was, I miss Christianity. Not the preaching, but all the splendid art and music that emerged from the Christian religion over the years. There's nothing of that here.'

Communication with the Chinese tower had been limited and terse for months. Much discussion had been taking place concerning the disgrace Phipp had brought to the West's relations with the Chinese. It was finally decided that a small delegation should go to the Chinese tower to apologise and, if the apology were accepted, to talk of closer relationships between the towers.

Phipp was restored to his role as door guardian, but only because no one else was available to take on the task. While this meant his release from confinement, Phipp, who had never been popular, had become shunned.

At a time when his drinking water had become inexplicably less than pure, Phipp strove to re-establish himself and remarked to Rooy, 'Water, the Bread of life . . .'

'He was groping blindly for profundity,' said Rooy, grinning. '"Water, the Bread of life . . ."' And with much laughter the quotation ascended the tower floor by floor until it reached the astronomers, amongst whom laughter was not greatly encouraged.

The fact was that once the existential thrill of actually being on a planet other than Earth had become blunted by custom, routine had set in. Routine and the dominating question of stillbirths had allowed 'boredom' – that withered word – to flourish.

16
Shap's Lecture

The morning Brightener in the West tower was occupied on a particular day by Shap, one of the women in Astronomy, speculating on the significance of the normon.

Shap patted her hair down before beginning her talk.

'Our terrible crisis here on Tharsis is, of course, the death of babies, the impossibility of life for them . . . The crisis appals our corporate mind like a dead child itself.

'But I must speak of the astroscience that is my occupation.'

Pausing, Shap patted her hair again, took a deep breath and began to talk in a less fluting voice.

'So, the normon. It takes a while for any new angle to be checked. The name itself may be changed. Various fresh tests have to be undergone before a paper appears in *Nature*. So far we have received support only from Chunderhof in New Delhi, where Knablo Mukurrji has arrived at the same understanding as we, in his researches. We are not talking Higgs Boson here.

'For a surprisingly long time, we humans have accepted that nothing can travel faster than light. However, we now believe this not to be the case, and that within – or let's say beside – light, there's a track relating to but separate from light, faster by far than light. That's our normon. It's more of a strip than a particle as we at first believed.

'Findings so far seem to show that a multiplicity of normons exist. We appear to have detected one that approaches Mars before veering off into the galaxy.'

One of Shap's listeners interrupted to say, 'So if you could travel by it, you might travel back in time?'

'We don't know as yet,' Shap responded. 'We do know, as someone once said, that the universe is strange, and stranger than we can imagine. It's a pity we still use the term "space" – very old-fashioned – for the great teeming ocean of particles surrounding us.'

She then became more technical, talking slowly, seeming to relish the minutiae of the research. Phipp left the chamber. Then another member followed, and another. Finally the talk was over and the remaining audience left the hall.

Noel had been listening with Troed, the chief engineer, and Iggog.

'She lacks lecture skills,' said Troed lightly, smiling.

Responding, Iggog said, 'The crowd was bored. You can easily learn a few lecture skills. A bit of humanity helps. She could have told us who this original Norman was.'

Noel paused outside her door. 'I trust you two realise that Shap was struggling with a concept – an enormously troubling concept . . . Well, it troubles me! She can see that if the hypothesis is correct, then we are not living in the universe we thought we were. We're living in a quite different universe.

'And my belief is that she struggles to conceal this idea, so as not to frighten the troops . . .'

17

Interlude: A Farewell To Families

One of those 'troops' was Tad, a fairly recent arrival, having landed on Mars on the convoy only just before Sheea's traumatic baby. His story had begun as mundanely as any other colonist's . . .

Tad Tadl and his partness, Ida Precious, stood in a cosy little room where plain nylon curtains hung down to a polished floor. On a small table in one corner were a squealer and a DTV set. Their home was in Reading, England. Outside, the big city's roar could be heard. By the tall window hung a cage containing a canary, staring out from its perch. The canary's wings fluttered slightly, as if it wished to escape from what it witnessed.

Tad and Ida, who were buying the house, were arguing with one another. Tad claimed that he had a hunger to see Mars. 'I'm the new generation! They've been there nearly ten years. The colonists are well-established by now.'

Ida had at first agreed, citing a fact she had read that development of eyes had promoted the dawn of intelligence, and it was intelligence that insisted the human race should occupy its neighbour in space. In species such as plants and fungi, among the innumerable eyeless types, intelligence had not evolved.

'That is the case, obviously,' Tad had said. 'It's only among the chordates you find intelligence. Who knows if, among the various bugs we inevitably take with us to Mars, intelligence may develop? Things are going to be different.'

'That's what's exciting. That's the lure,' she *had* said.

Tad put a hand on Ida's breast and made greedy gobbling noises.

The hand of a man, the paw of a bear, the wing of a bird, all have an evolutionary relationship, all serve purposeful behaviour. But on the Moon, only the hand of man is to be found.

A Western recession was now in its third year, growing deeper, afflicting even bank managers. Shoots to the Moon had in consequence been cut from once every six months to once every ten. Tad had booked their flight long ago, on one of those new graceful Chinese space planes. Now he was embarking on the Moon lift without Ida. He tried not to think of her.

In recent days she had become silent. Tad had done his best to draw her out; Ida had closed her eyes and shaken her head. She would not accept his embraces.

Finally, she had burst into speech. 'It's no good. I don't want to go to bloody Mars! Why should anyone want to go to bloody Mars? Have they got coffee shops there? Movies? Gardens, streets, hotels? Music? Anything living or lively? Not a bit of it! Sorry, Tad – you go alone if you must!'

And she had a job in a lousy bank.

He found himself now seated in a crowded vehicle. Men and women were there, mainly in the twenties-to-forties age range. Few of them talked, some held hands, all were aware of the challenge of the enterprise on which they were already embarking.

While the complex mass of energy-driven proteins and fats constituting their brains held knowledge of the adventure in which they would play their part, their bodies were tense with apprehension. The lunar vehicle pulsed with it.

The passengers, men and women, had already exchanged their own currencies for UU tokens. Farewells to families had been made and those embraces were finished with. They had already begun a final departure from Earth.

The Moon was a busy place. The side facing Earth was littered with speedroads and factories and tourist hotels. It was estimated that something close to four million people now lived on the Moon for periods of not more than a statutory ninety days – a period in which health was not undermined by the light gravity.

Tad Tadl and those who had travelled up with him were lodged in the spartan Adios Hotel, in the city-nexus of Armstrong. Here, meals were graded to become more parsimonious day by day.

Tad's family had come to say farewell to him and watch the big launch. His two younger brothers were bubbling with excitement and envy. His mother was choking back tears, but complimented him adoringly on his courage. Father, Tad's beaky-nosed father, had been told not to exercise his disapproval of the entire project. A powerful-looking man, he nevertheless did what his wife told him. 'A sad loss to the family, old boy,' was the nearest he got to voicing his feelings. Tad patted his father's back. 'I never did please you, pop. You'll sleep easy once I'm out the way.'

'Indeed we won't, love,' said mother. Father said nothing. He blinked rapidly. With the rocket launched, Tad's mother burst into tears.

And when the crying ceased, her sense of something missing from her life continued.

On Luna, while awaiting the Mars craft in its orbit, the would-be exiles exercised and were lectured to.

Their main lecturer was a plump and cheerful man, by name Morgan Reece. Over his large torso was draped a T-shirt, the message on which read 'SAME OLD SHIT? NO – DIFFERENT SHIT'.

'Yes, I'm lucky Morgan Reece, and I will retain both parts of my name,' he said. 'You will all lose your surname; some may be given new names assigned by computer, the easier to keep tabs on you in your new existence. Also, this way, you are less likely to think of your families. Homesickness doesn't pay off. You'll be on your way to Mars within the week, when your birth names will remain behind as kind of ghost-memories of your earthly existence.

'That goes for you too, Tompkins, dear . . .

'Right now, I'm taking the opportunity to tell you about things which you may already know. Bear with me.

'I will start by quoting a twentieth century philosopher, Bertram Russell – who has left both his names behind. The good Bertram said, "Man is the product of causes which had no prevision of the end they were achieving". Quite so. Otherwise, we might fly to the planets on gossamer wings. As it is, we are flying blind, evolution-wise. Don't imagine further development has come to a grinding halt, because that just ain't how the system works.

'One of the reasons you lot are schlepping off to Mars is because you can no longer bear to believe in things that just ain't so. Unlike most of the nutcases around here.

'*Someone* died for our sins over two thousand years ago. Well, that one hasn't worked out, has it?

'Think big. You already think big in confronting a perilous trip into unknown difficulties. I hope to add to your stature by talking about the universe itself. Mind and intelligence are under threat. China has to confront nuclear aggression from North Korea. Ingushetia has been reduced to ruin. The Libyans have accidentally blown themselves up – could happen to anyone, provided they were stupid enough. The lovely island of Bali has become a battleground.

'A large part of Westminster Abbey has been destroyed by a suicide-bomber, as you know. Almost unreported, Hungary, Slovakia and Bulgaria are at war. There is civil war again in Ireland. Need I go on? Bitter tribal wars continue in Somalia, the Congo and elsewhere. This is yet another Dark Age among the many of the past. Stupidity seems to prevail.

'And yet we know how precious intelligence is, how men have fought for its continuance over the ages. To manage to quit this Earth is an act of courage and intelligence. Why is the operation so difficult? Why, we ask after two centuries of searching, is a minor little planet like our Earth the only home of intelligence? As far as we know, that is, despite all the guessing games we're good at.'

Morgan Reece paused for a moment, chewing over how he might put across his next point most effectively.

'And if all this really is the case, then it implies – no, it means – that all the stars in the universe, which number about ten billion trillion, exist for the sake of our intelligence and our limited way of life only. Come on, who're you kidding?

'In my next lecture, I shall be more technical – this is just an introduction to that torture. But we can see that the size of the galaxy is related to the length of time of its existence. That's time enough for there to be plenty of carbon around. Carbon provides the basis for all life forms. Is that by design, or did it just so happen?

'There is less oxygen than carbon in circulation. Which is as well, I'd say, or otherwise, catching fire from the sun, the whole scheme of things might go up in smoke.

'From our point of view, it is a misfortune that Mars has no oxygen, whatever was the case in the past. There is much we do not yet understand. By living on Mars you will discover much more. Understand more.

'No oxygen, no water. Until this last century and the intolerable over-population of our world, water was plentiful here on Earth. And just think – water is a contradiction of nature. Generally speaking, solid forms are heavier than liquid or gaseous forms of the same material. Not so with water. Ice is lighter than water. Isn't that weird? Isn't it something more than just lucky?

'Were it otherwise, in cold water the ice when it formed would sink. The coldest water, becoming heavier, would also sink. Thus ice would accumulate. Oceans would become solid ice. And so in a matter of years, we would have a frozen world, on which intelligence, life itself, would be impossible.

'Does this mean that certain chemical reactions have been skewed so that we can live? It's a big, big question. Why used young lads to leave their homes to go a-wandering? To discover the big world, of course. As you all are about to do.

'Same old shit? No, like I say, "Different Shit" . . .'

Tad wondered what a bank contributed to any higher form of

knowledge. He thought longingly of Ida. Soon, she and her wretched bank would be millions of miles away.

Everyone was losing a lover or a family.

Finally this body of men and women was lifted from the city of Armstrong to the orbiting space vehicle *Confu*. The *Confu* weighed ninety hundred tons, almost twice the weight of the RMS *Titanic*, which had sunk centuries earlier.

The real significance of this operation still echoed the confidence and consternation caused by the departure of the first colonising ship for the Red Planet – some years back now – to carry a brave freight of the elite and adventurous who had signed away any chance of returning to their natal planet. Yes, they faced hardship but, no, not decline.

Many an onlooker was unable to decide whether this long farewell marked a loss or a gain in the terrestrial story. The future itself posed something of the same dilemma: those of a more pessimistic nature looked towards it with gloom, while the optimists anticipated good things to materialise. As far as terrestrial activities went, there was justification for both views.

Defying fate – especially the fate of others – a band stood in the main square of Armstrong, playing martial music as the ferry rose, among which uplifting airs 'It's a Long Way to Tipperary' was deemed particularly appropriate.

No crowds cheered to say farewell at the start of this historic voyage. The lungs of a multitude would have taxed the production of breathable air. Only the eyes of instruments recorded the epoch-making launch.

The ferry carried the new exiles from Armstrong up to the *Confu*, waiting in orbit. The group boarded the great vessel, to find it not entirely as they had expected. This new design of ship held, below the engine room, a small ferry craft. At the right moment, when the *Confu* was in orbit round Mars, the small ferry would take the exiles down to their new home, together with necessary supplies of UU medicines, fuel and food. So the *Confu* could return for an overhaul in its orbit above Armstrong, to be used over again.

The *Confu*. Their quarters were spartan and situated in the heart of the ship, as proofed as could be against the destructive powers of radiation. First came a curved-wall living space; it was like living in an egg, as someone remarked. This room led into sleeping quarters with much gleaming apparatus looming above each bunk.

Some of the voluntary exiles regarded their protective suiting as too heavy, but the yixiing huaheng suiting had useful qualities. It never wore out and it served as partial protection against radiation.

The exiles lay at right angles to the direction of flight. Under the space suits, worn most of the time, was fitted a liquid conditioning garment, relieving the heat generated by the body and conducting it to a heater for coffee, enjoyed during the rare breaks of consciousness on the journey.

'Gee, it's ingenious!' one woman exclaimed.

'I'd say primitive,' said another.

'Primitive? Wait till you hit Mars!' a girl relabelled Iggog said.

The adjoining third chamber was a gym, loaded with equipment. Off the gym was a stub of passageway leading to shower-rooms and W.C.s. Everything, as they soon decided, was decidedly cramped. But clever.

But there they were. And they were already on their way.

A hushed recorded voice told them of their routine. A light meal, then enforced sleep period, then enforced awakening, then forced exercise. Followed by optional shower under recycled liquid. Then a light meal, then enforced sleep, then enforced awakening, then forced exercise.

And so on, over and over, the exercise periods gradually growing more demanding. Scenes from Mars would be shown on the screen in the living room – scenes lasting for four minutes.

Some exiles began to feel like experimental animals. On that protracted journey, Tad who'd kept his own first name, was haunted by dreams in which, it seemed, he had lived a long time ago. He and his comrades sailed a wine-dark sea rich with monsters. The crew responded to a brisk following wind and the gulls cried, shrill as the wind.

The men hauled up the mast, making it fast with stays. They

hoisted the bellying brown sail, securing it with ropes. And all the while he stood over them, long hair caught in any breeze, beaky-nosed like his father, scowling at the wave hissing round their stern.

They sped through the choppy seas, forging ahead for ever.

And never a sight of land, of Ithaca.

18

Interlude Part II: A Long Journey and A Short Walk

That long journey had been taken by human beings many times before. The towers were filling. Mars was no longer as it had been.

Coverage of the launch had figured largely on all squealers and shriekers. Gradually the interest stirred up dissipated. Humanity went back to teaching others to behave, to watching football matches, to being good people, to being holy, to fighting each other, to collecting old books, to reading new ones, to composing poetry, to getting drunk and drugged, to painting and sculpting, to respecting and despising or loving others, to thinking, to fantasising, to finding someone suitable or unsuitable with whom to copulate, to being ill or kind or clever or positively unbearable, to laughing and crying, to dying. All the things it was possible to do.

Only on the *Confu* were impossible things being done.

The passengers were roused in shifts of six at a time. They were exercised before being allowed a twenty minute break of consciousness. In that time, they sat and drank coffee heated by their own blood temperature. And talked. Or sat silent.

'I've longed to get to Mars. I've not had much of a success in life.' A man called Ficht was talking, rather a sorry figure, stooped and with a look of fatigue about him; yet when he spoke he was succinct enough. 'I'm an astronomer. Viewing should be excellent on Mars. I hope to be a success for a change. Or at least to learn something.'

He looked at the man next to him. 'I suppose you despise me after what I've said. What do you do in life?'

'I'm Doran. I don't care what you say, chief! Spill your beans . . . Spent most of my time recently on what's left of the Ross Ice Shelf. I used to draw comic strips. I used to love a sweet blonde wench.'

'Waste of time, I'd say,' said a third man, Haddod. 'You aren't suffering from SNA already, are you?'

Ignoring this remark, Doran said, in a leisurely kind of way, 'I woke up this time thinking how quickly we learn things. Think of comic strips – I used to draw one called "Petty Proceedings". You know you mainly draw things in little boxes. One little box can carry you into the next box just a microsecond along in the characters' lives. Or maybe a million years. Funny, isn't it? So your eyes move just one small space to the next box and you can be a microsecond along or a million years. We suss all that pretty damn quick. Isn't that clever of us?'

'You soon get used to it,' said Haddod.

'But isn't that what I'm saying? We do a learning curve pretty damn quick.'

Ficht was more sympathetic. 'So, space is made to equal time. In other words, it's like this trip to Mars we're taking. Any time, the gong will go. We sleep. We wake and a thousand – two thousand – or is it three thousand? – miles of space have disappeared.'

As he finished the mild gong sounded. They smiled at each other and nodded. Comic strip boxes. Trips to Mars . . .

They all climbed back into their bunks. This brief spell of consciousness was over.

Being born is the most convenient, conventional, way of joining a family. It is not the only way; one can join a welcoming family without undergoing one's childhood in it. And equally one can get kicked out of a family. Nevertheless, the family has proved durable throughout the ages. In the animal kingdom, matters differ from one species to another. Elephants observe family connections. Young tigers growing up leave their family for good. The necessity to hunt and eat exercises a strong influence. Even a poor human family will sit and share fish and chips or a pizza round the screamer. One does not have to be happy in a family. To cohere or adhere is often sufficient.

So it was with the new bank manager. With her lover on his way to Mars, Ida Precious returned to the Precious family; that is, to her old parents, her two brothers, who played musical instruments for a living of sorts, and her younger sister, Ivy, of sulky disposition, working in the Complaints Department of a large chain of furniture retailers. If a cushion split or a leg fell off a sofa, you would most likely find yourself talking to Ivy.

The Precious house was roomy, roomy enough to contain a lodger in one of the back rooms. This lodger's name was Mike Maplethorp, of religious but blithe nature, and it was to Mike that Ida found herself inclining in the evenings, when she returned from the rustle of bank notes and the persecution of debtors . . . Indeed, it was Mike the lodger who persuaded Ida that her sense of guilt at abandoning Tad Tadl could be assuaged by visiting the local church of a Sunday.

So when the congregation was not singing hymns, she sat, elegant behind one wooden pew, with her head bowed, sometimes holding Mike's hand. She listened to the vicar telling the congregation wildly unlikely things, such as that God had spent seven days creating the world, or that Jesus, dying on the Cross, had saved generations over two thousand years later from Sin. It puzzled her that such stories were still put about. Presumably it was not yet illegal.

Thanks to Mike's prompting, the vicar singled out Ida as she was leaving the outer door. He was a man of medium build, rather gaunt, in his forties and already with some grey hair showing. He was bony of face, but with a kindly look to him. He approached her in a flurry of black and white skirts.

'I hope I don't encroach too greatly on your thoughts, but you have a troubled look, my dear. If I can be of any help to you . . .'

The look she flashed him was not entirely unfriendly. 'It's quite all right, thank you.'

'Our Saviour is always by our side when we need him. He will comfort us.'

She glanced about her but saw no one.

'I was speaking metaphorically, miss. Really our entire lives are a metaphor until we come to the glory of His presence. That will be our promised reality. Then we shall see Him face to face.'

Ida wanted to ask how long they would have to stand there staring, but instead said merely, 'I'm afraid I don't believe all that. When we're dead, we're dead, and that's the end of it.'

'Ah, now I understand why your face is full of sorrow.'

They were walking along a path fringed with plants. The roses sprawling on their right hand side were particularly beautiful. Beyond the bed of flowers were gravestones, some dating back three centuries, their stones carved with loving words: 'always in our hearts', 'much loved', 'wife of the above', 'never forget you'. Those who had had the phrases carved had themselves now departed, to be forgotten by following generations.

Glancing slyly at the vicar, Ida said, 'I am sad for a rather worldly reason. My boyfriend is on his way to Mars without me. At the last moment, I refused to go along too.'

'Then you are greatly to be praised, my dear,' said the vicar. A pigeon meandered on the path just ahead of the pair of them. It barely eluded the episcopal shoes before lumbering unharmed into the air. With scarcely a break in his speech, the vicar continued. 'Cursed are all they who try to leave this world that God hath blessed. Remember in the Good Book it says, "And Isaac went out to meditate in the field at the eventide; and he lifted up his eyes and saw . . ." So we may lift up our eyes and see Mars, but to wish to walk there is a sin . . . God gave us this world to walk upon. He had no word to say about walking on unhallowed worlds. You may well sorrow for the sin of your young man!'

She groaned. 'Apologies, but you have it all wrong, Vicar! What I regret is my own behaviour – that instead of joining my man I took the materialist point of view to seize on promotion at work. And that a lousy bank.'

At the gate of the churchyard, the Vicar said gently, 'Come again and pray with us, my dear, and your way will be made clear.'

'Unfortunately it's all too clear as it is: I have been mercenary. But thanks.'

Ida went on her way, saying to herself, 'Oh god! . . . But what a nice man.'

19

The Vexed Question of Umwelts

Among the most intelligent exiles on Tharsis was the woman now known as 'Vooky'. She had been the Professor of Philosophy in the university nearest the North Pole. It was her duty on Tharsis to worry about things, and to record those worries on the UU screech, just in case they might be useful at some future date.

Vooky worried about the stillbirth problem, although that problem had officials investigating it. But still she worried, indeed grieved, since she had borne one of the first dying children. Ever since then, she had listened acutely to what other grieving mothers said about the situation.

The remark she found most concerning was the resigned, 'It was meant to be', which sounded to Vooky like the potential birth of a religion.

On this particular day, she was brooding over a statement set in the mouth of 'Rasselas, Prince of Abissinia". In Samuel Johnson's novel of that name, the Prince addresses a man who is mourning the death of his daughter. He says, 'Consider that external things are naturally variable, but truth and reason are always the same.'

Loath to believe that Johnson could be mistaken, Vooky took a walk outside the settlement. She invited her secretary to follow her, which the secretary did, and followed without saying a word, for fear of disturbing Vooky's line of thought.

Over the cold shield and a little to the south Vooky walked. She missed her collie dog, so loving and intelligent, which she had been forced to leave behind. It was now understood that dogs, cats and pigs possessed at the least their own kind of intelligence and intuitions. It was accepted that the old nursery tales with their talking wolves and bears were something more than light-headed fantasy. Such understandings formed part of the current intellectual umwelt, the environment of the understanding. For much of the span of human existence, human concepts – their umwelts – which presided over their affairs, had remained limited. For instance, the term 'universe' had for a long time been limited to a concept where the Earth was stationary and remained the centre of everything: and everything where the stars were simply points of light on a ceiling.

Now the learned part of the world had vaulted itself into a new environment. Perhaps it carried its umwelt on its shoulders. Again she struggled with her own mind, to escape from something, something that she was unable to identify.

Yoga . . . was it only in meditation one could escape from whatever the current imprisoning was?

Such cogitations gained a splutter of new life when Vooky and her secretary happened on an old robotruck, all but buried under driven sand and heterogeneous material, and parked behind a curtain of lava rock.

'My god,' exclaimed Vooky. 'Give me a hand, will you . . .'

The two of them scraped some regolith away. Vooky climbed into the cabin of the truck. Some of its instruments remained operative. Vooky knew the vehicle was of historic interest – even a decade on such a young colony was a long time; it was the machine that had been used by those hydrologists, Prestwick and Simpson, in their reconnaissance, the exploration on which the entire Martian venture had depended. Though scarcely acknowledged now, it was their discoveries that had made the UU venture a viable proposition.

The secretary reminded Vooky that both men had died returning to Earth.

Fiddling with a bank of switches, Vooky lit up an account of a long-dead woman's life. This strange woman, who had at first been called Theodora, had struck up a friendship with an abbot. This and her remarkable holiness formed the basis of a kind of biography. It was puzzling, incomprehensible.

This strange Theodora had changed her name to Christina. She swore to remain chaste, untouched by mortal man – and she wasn't lesbian. She thought of herself as a 'Bride of Christ.' This was in the twelfth century AD.

Christina had undergone many hardships, as detailed in this account, which was entitled *A Life of Christina of Markyate*. Twelfth century! What could life have been like then . . .? 'You shudder to think,' she said to herself. 'Hideous!'

Here was an entire umwelt of bygone beliefs, mostly mistaken to Vooky's mind, and yet, in its small enclosed way, working well enough. Everyone believed in its tenets. So they went almost unnoticed, each in their time.

Truth and reason were not inevitably the same.

So she had caught Johnson in a philosophical mistake. She was both proud and ashamed – ashamed at her self-congratulatory glow of discovery.

'Uhhh,' she exclaimed, realising she had wet herself in her excitement. A dribble only; it would soon dry. The small indignities imposed by Mars had been worsened by her childbirth that was all loss and no reward.

She had observed somewhere that at the very beginnings of space flight, when a small sample of mankind had landed on the Moon, there were many who swore it had never happened; unwilling to move to a new umwelt. Now there were the stubborn ones who claimed that Mars was still uninhabitable, preferring the lie to a new umwelt.

All over Earth – wasn't that at the heart of the problem? – Different umwelts were scattered, each one confidently believing its own kind of truth, each bruising the others with their differences.

Nowadays it was accepted – and Vooky accepted it – that there were multiverses. But what was truth? The binary system – that, she thought, in the history of man's search for knowledge was a relatively new truth. And at least half the cretins down on Earth refused to believe it even now.

Those exiles who had removed themselves from the umwelts of Earth had been escaping from god and religion.

Truth and reason were necessarily identical. Vooky switched off the curious document. She and her secretary began the plod home, to report their discovery of the old robotruck.

Another sand gale was brewing. 'Perhaps we can rescue the truck and get it into working order again,' said the secretary, glancing through her mask at Vooky. 'It would be useful, wouldn't it?'

She added, 'And we'd be celebrated . . .'

Vooky gave no answer.

She had discovered a new thing to worry about.

20
A Troubled Exwo

Aymee and Rooy were taking their traditional stroll over the eternal twilights close to the settlement. The silence pleased them. Only now and again did something occur to them as they walked. Aymee was remarking with a chuckle, 'Think of all the industry and machinery it took to land us here. And you could say we're back in a pastoral setting!'

He clasped her arm to halt her.

Their eyes had adjusted to the near-dark; they clearly saw the figure lying sprawled ahead of them. They were astonished. They hurried over to it.

The figure wore an air mask. As Aymee was about to take the man's pulse, the figure rolled over and said weakly, 'Dying . . . my Maker. Following our Saviour.' He began to choke, his air supply failing.

Rooy pulled off his own mask, and alternated holding it to the other man's face then his own, so that they could take turns having access to oxygen. The man groaned. Struggling, he managed the words, 'Too late.'

'Let's get him on our shoulders and drag him home.' As Rooy was speaking, he heaved the man more or less upright. Aymee flung one of his dangling arms over her shoulder, and together they got him into a more-or-less vertical position.

He was half-walking, knees knocking together, mainly being dragged. He began to sob. They heard him crying, gulping down his sobs. 'I was following Jesus . . .' he managed to say. 'Jesus ahead. Me – me following . . .'

They got him to the West tower gate, rang for re-admittance. Rooy was panting.

Phipp opened up, to stare in surprise at the trio. He looked more closely at the figure Rooy was propping up.

'He's one of those Exwos,' he said.

'Just get through the test, will you?' said Aymee. 'We need a doctor. This man almost died.'

The three got themselves into the elevator. It carried them to the little emergency ward on the second floor. The man groaned when they stripped off most of his clothes and put him on a bed; an air mask was clamped over his head. Rooy was given an improvised armchair and a pipe of oxygen.

As soon as Aymee was satisfied that both men were being cared for, she nodded farewell to her partner and began to turn back towards her suite on the second floor.

'Hang on, I'm not dead yet,' said Rooy, heaving himself up. He caught Aymee's hand. She turned a relieved face to him. They kissed each other.

Later, Rooy took the elevator down into the depths, where he worked among the E&M (Electronics and Machines) which kept the tower functional.

His first task on this day was to incinerate a malformed baby corpse – and keep quiet about it.

On Aymee's door was a small notice saying,

TELL ME YOUR TROUBLES   AYMEE CLINIC

106

She was researching early files on the truck Vooky had discovered when there was a tap on her door.

A large man in overalls was waiting nervously to speak to her. Short hair stood stiffly on his head. He had an artificial pearl dangling from his left ear. Aymee led him into her tiny inner sanctum, where she offered him a cup of coffee. He relaxed somewhat.

'I was given to understand you was a psychotherapist, miss. Is that so? And that you saved me, out on the Shield.'

'Oh, I'm sorry, I didn't recognise you. You were a tad worse for wear. You have made a rapid recovery.'

'Providence, ma'am. You and your partner were sent to rescue me. The Lord did not wish me to die. He still has work for me to do.'

Aymee looked puzzled. 'What lord to you mean? Not the Director?'

'The Lord God, ma'am. The Lord who rules over us all.'

She was vexed.

'Let me have your name first of all.'

'Oh, I'm Herb, miss.' He spoke, she thought, with some pride.

She clicked it into her squealer. 'You can call me Aymee.'

Ignoring the suggestion, Herb said, 'I'm an Exwo, miss. Or I was. The Lord sent me here to Mars to do odd jobs.'

Aymee knew well enough what an Exwo was. To relieve the high rate of unemployment on Earth, or at least to appear to relieve it, and to make economically useless people useful on Tharsis, a number of unemployed men had been sent out from Earth. The order which had made this possible proved unpopular locally. All other 'settlers' on Mars were strictly volunteers, who regarded the Exwos as being of low mental calibre. But they had, in their way, been as deliberately selected as any.

'This is too much like Britain in the past sending criminals to Australia,' Mangalian had said.

Flights to Mars had by this time become commonplace. Yet somehow an accident had occurred on a space plane used to transport five hundred "ex-workers". All but three men had died en route and two of those had died after landing. The shipyard on Luna had been nationalised and the accident had been hushed up, so that other potential travellers were not deterred from making the journey.

Herb viewed her steadily over the rim of his mug as she thought.

'So, Herb, you are the only Exwo who made it here . . . I guess you have not yet entirely taken to the experience?' Aymee said, keeping sarcasm from her voice.

'The Lord had reason to spare me.'

'And to have all the other men die?'

He barely shrugged. 'The Lord moves in a mysterious way.'

She was annoyed by this smugness. 'My notice invites you to tell me your troubles, so I gather that this Lord of yours needs some help occasionally.'

'I am called to return to Earth.'

She told him that that could not be done. Returns to Earth were for freight, and to reuse the carriers. While the Exwo contracts were different to those of the volunteers, they could not return home before their allocated time – there were no suitable ships.

He appeared unperturbed. 'There's a man called Barrin back on Earth,' Herb said. 'How did he get back there? And he's coming back here again, I hear. Or supposed to be. So why not others?'

'Barrin was special – and celebrated – and the journey to Earth made him gravely ill. He died before he could return here.'

Herb paid no attention to this remark. He went into a story about how his family owned a boathouse on the River Nene. His family had been makers of small boats for years. 'Willows and mud and river water – that's what we been used to.' But there had been a fire in which all was lost. His father had lost his life, trying to put out the blaze; when they came to claim the insurance, the courts ruled that Herb's father had committed suicide. His father had not been religious.

'Everything's against you in life, miss.'

'We may sometimes say that here on Tharsis, in the light of a good deal of tangible evidence, because what we call circumstances appear to be against us. But it's an attitude we hope to overcome. Talking of a god is not going to help. We need to look after ourselves.'

'Sorry, miss – everything *is* against you, whatever you may claim, when you don't even have a priest here.'

Aymee took a moment to consider whether to refute Herb's claim. 'There are many people who become entrenched in an attitude which will prove unhelpful, barring them perhaps from the achievement of a more resilient and consequently happier life. All of us at one time or another may feel that things are against us. But to continue to consider ourselves as being perennially the victims of adversity is to dig ourselves a trench from which we may ultimately find ourselves unable to escape. In other words, it is not this rather fictional 'everything' that sinks us: it is our own perversity.'

Herb hunched his shoulders and shrugged his hands.

'You use all them big words. But they don't worry me. I'm not such a fool as I look. The Lord is my shepherd.'

'I was hoping to help. Life is hard here, but rewarding. And you're not a sheep.'

'Jesus!' he exclaimed, slapping his forehead. 'Look, miss, there's no rivers here on Mars, is there? How can you bear a place without rivers? I'm falling sick. I know it. I feel it in me bones. The Lord needs me to get back to Earth. Possibly start up my old trade again. By a river, okay?'

'I'm afraid there are laws, Herb. An Exwo may not return to Earth for eight years, Earth years. You'll have to try and make the best of things. You might find you even enjoy it here. I do not wish to be rude, but you must forget all this troublesome business about God.'

'It's not fair. I seen them used supply rockets lying about near to here in the desert. Can't we send me home in one of those?'

'We have no way of launching used supply rockets. I'm afraid you will have to adjust to our way of life here. Come and talk to me again in a month, and we'll see how you get on.'

For the first time, Herb showed impatience. 'God gives me powers others do not have, prophetic powers, for instance. One day, strange people with strange voices will land here and show powers you never dreamed of. I need to leave before then.' He gave a curt little bow and left, slamming Aymee's door behind him.

All these brief human lives were being lived out as part of the great drama of the century, the arrival of groups of people on another world, the long-dreamed-of world of Mars. Even the knowledge that humanity lived in a binary system did not greatly alter matters.

The burly man with an artificial pearl in his left ear was fortunate. All he wanted was to go home. Aymee and Rooy talked the conversation over. Rooy laughed. 'Cheeky blighter! All his talk about God was to scare you into getting him back to Earth!'

'What about these aliens he claims will arrive?'

'Oh, the idiot was only trying to frighten you.' He hugged her to him.

When Herb had removed himself from Aymee's office, Aymee had sat staring into space, remembering unbidden a time on earth when her parents had taken her from the West for a holiday in Rajasthan. They had stayed by a tributary of the River Karai. There, she and her little sister had had their fill of 'willows and mud and river water', as Herb had put it.

Oh yes, and the flowers there, flowers on the bank, flowers of a deep reddish gold, tiny forests of them. And the butterflies.

Ah, those butterflies . . .

But it was useless to be nostalgic. There was this newly discovered hydrologists' truck to be hauled up to the towers.

21
Images of the Past

The Brighteners were at risk of becoming less and less cheerful. The topic of childbirth was avoided, but only replaced with complaints about other bodily functions failing.

'We all have to put up with various aches and pains,' Noel said. 'We know that you men all suffered from constipation and testicular pain for a long while after your journeys here.'

Ooma added in her deep husky voice, 'Also, Noel, some of us ladies have been suffering from what we know as "dim-eye", simply because the sunlight is rather attenuated. The retina tends to drop into sleep mode.'

'Quite so. Thank you, Ooma,' said Noel kindly. 'In fact – I hate to tell you this – it is possible we are developing new aches, advanced cateracts, for instance, individual to Mars. Mind-clutter, too. That thing we christened SNA – Suppressed Nostalgia Affliction. Many of us suffer from a kind of mental conflict, part of us wanting to remember a peaceful scene from our childhood on Earth, or perhaps our first love affair, and so on.

'And on the other hand, wishing not to remember – something delightful, something hateful, an aberrant form of home-sickness. Doesn't matter, not to SNA – because it simply will not help us here on Tharsis, where we have determined to live out our destiny.'

Ooma mentioned something about her predecessor's poem, but it was Aymee who interrupted. 'Surely there is something – well, if not healing, then at least soothing, regarding the past. About an hour ago, I was remembering a river in Rajasthan with beautiful flowers on its banks. That did me no harm.'

'But if you pined for it?' Noel said.

'Well, it was poignant, admittedly. But a five-minute pine should not hurt anyone.' She laughed, as did several others round the table.

Daark spoke later, bringing up the one hope for the problem of the stillbirths – that it might fade out as physiologies adjusted to the lighter Martian gravity. 'An evolutionary change, you might call it. But evolutionary changes often happen surprisingly rapidly.' An instance Daark gave was how soon the tusks of African elephants had shrunk in response to poachers killing them for their ivory.

He changed the topic, clearly uncomfortable speaking about it for long. 'Another notion just mentioned we might use to our general benefit. No reason why Earth memories should atrophy. Let's have a series of sessions of formal reminiscences of past incidents in our lives on Earth. Record them. I left behind a wife and children, which I feel bad about. Such sessions could be curative. Everyone allowed just – oh, I don't know, let's say fifteen minutes. We don't want life stories.'

There was general agreement that Daark's suggestion was a good one.

'Those lovely flowers of yours,' said Thirn, overcoming her shyness to address Aymee. 'They may not be on that river bank any more, sad to say.'

Tad, who was a night-soil supervisor, continued, 'In memory, those flowers did you no harm. But you must know that after the recent Indi-Rajasthan disturbances, when so many homes and lives were wantonly destroyed, your riverbank flowers are probably no more. Obvious grounds for SNA, in my book.'

'Whatever has happened since, my memory remains a happy one.' said Aymee. Yet inwardly, knowing the district had been so stricken, she was less sure than she pretended.

Someone asked Noel, 'How about looking forward? Is that as bad as looking back?'

'Even worse, I'd guess,' said Noel, amid a few chuckles round the table.

The old derelict surveyors' truck was dragged into the open space in front of the six towers. There was some puzzled interest in the recording about the 'Bride of Christ'. A service of a kind was held, to which all were invited, and the names of the two surveyors evoked.

This was used as an excuse to resume communication with all the other towers. After Phipp's incident with the Chinese, colonists in the other towers had been more aloof. Nearly a year later, they still seldom initiated conversation with the West. Now, a conference was called, in a room dedicated to inter-tower video communications. It moved almost immediately from the topic of the surveyors to that which was preying on every mind.

Russ-East spoke straightforwardly of the failure to produce living babies. 'In fact, for two months all sexual intercourse was forbidden here. As a result of demonstrations, we had to allow intercourse again, but strict contraceptive measures are now in force. We realise this does not solve this terrible issue. Please keep in touch.'

The Singa-Thai tower was more cautious. 'We admit sadly we have only stillbirths to report so far. We have been cautious regarding talk of this matter, believing that we had here some kind of viral disease. Our gynaecologists are still investigating the problem. If you have definite results, stay in touch. We are pleased to speak with you on this painful subject.'

The Scand tower admitted that fifty-nine babies had been delivered. All badly malformed, all dying within five minutes of birth. Their gynaecologists believed this unanticipated disaster to be caused by the mothers being unaccustomed to lighter gravity. They had little hope for future normalisation. They suggested that if only one male and one female child could survive to maturity, they would mate and produce a perfectly normal series of children, or by then

– as they put it – wombs would have acclimatised. But such was only speculation.

The Sud-Am tower said that they were too shocked to discuss the matter. They had now reverted to religion and prayer, seeing religion as the one hope for survival. A woman called Sue Souto spoke of the power of prayer, walking to and fro in a nervous way, in a kind of greenhouse.

'God bless us all in this awful world,' she said in conclusion.

As Sud-Am cut off, Daze, watching from Sheea's knee, squealed, 'That was a birdie in there, mummy. I heard it!'

'Of course it wasn't,' said her mother. 'It was just something in the camera, squeaking.'

Daze shook her little fists in emphasis. 'I know it was a birdie. I was born on Earth, where lots of birds are everywhere.'

It was Ooma who first spoke up for the girl, and then others in the audience agreed they too had heard the chirp of a bird.

'If that is the case,' said Noel, 'it's another serious breach of our UU agreement. "No Pets", that's the rule we established.'

One of the men remarked that it might be a comfort for a pregnant woman to have a bird or a cat for company by her bed. Women were like that, whatever the rules.

A young brightly painted woman from Records said, 'You men, you don't know what we go through!'

But she was told this was a sexist remark, not encouraged within the confines of the settlement.

Noel gave an order to the compoutat for all top medical staff not already present to join the conference. 'There's another guideline we should observe – not to interfere with the activities of another tower unless invited.'

To her audience she said, 'We have to face realities. We are good at facing realities. You might say we came to Mars to face realities. Well, here's a real reality for us. We must focus on the facts or we'll never solve the problem. We are not alone in this catastrophe. New-born babies cannot live on Tharsis. That's the truth of it. At present at least.

'Our sad little corpses are preserved in the mortuary or outside. We will issue a thorough medical report on the matter as soon as possible. And of course – I must remind you – you are not allowed in the mortuary.'

A young woman called Tuot said, 'I am pregnant. I think I am prepared to face the facts but I would like to be clear about what the facts really are.'

Even as she spoke, even as the man sitting next to her reached for and held her hand, three doctors spoke together.

They addressed the company, admitting there was as yet no cure for the infant deaths in sight.

'Dear Tuot,' one of them said, 'we shall do everything we can for you. Let's have a chat and an examination after the meeting.'

'Me too, please,' said another young woman, blushing.

'And me,' said a third.

These young ladies had been what had become known as 'flooring'. Originally, the term had been 'third flooring'. The West tower had never attempted to ban sex. It was agreed, however, that sexual matters might be formalised, and a number of comfortable little nooks had been arranged for such necessary occasions. These were on the third floor. Since the nooks were frequently used, so the term for them had been abbreviated. Flooring had decreased since Noel's announcement; the prospect of delivering a deformed and dead infant proved a deterrent to copulation, to men almost as much as to women. Almost, but not quite.

22

Phipp has Problems to Share

Everyone departed silently from the conference except for one middle-aged man, a heavy red-cheeked man with what looked like a pronounced pout. He took Noel by her upper arm.

'May I have a word privately?' He gave her his attempt at an engaging smile. She shook off his clutch.

Many people lingered in the corridor. The man followed Noel at a short distance, so that no one should notice him with her. She led him into her office, closing the door behind him.

'I recognise you. You're one of the guards at the gate, aren't you? Is your name Phillip?'

'Phipp, ma'am, Phipp. Yes, I guard the gate and am proud to do so.' He stabbed at his chest with a thumb. 'I don't stand no nonsense.'

'I can see you have no manners.' She was annoyed that he had touched her so familiarly.

Phipp put on a hangdog look.

'It's a vital function, lady. Look, I got a serious problem bugging me.'

For once, Noel's calm demeanour cracked. She was shaken by the appalling implications of the news from the other towers.

'Oh, you have something bugging you? Well then, bad luck! I guess you don't figure a mortuary full of dead babies is a serious problem?'

He stared at her in astonishment, before spreading hands wide and saying, 'So? Dead planet, dead babies . . .'

'Get out of here!' she shrieked. Then, remembering her secondary role as advisor, she regained her composure long enough to suggest he came back a few hours later.

Phipp had shown himself to be a conscientious guardian of the gate. The main aspect of his job was to see that the automatic medical tests were working correctly. But that was only a day job, since no settlers remained outside after dark. There was also a rougher aspect of the job, more to Phipp's taste. Single men, single women, sometimes couples, took it into their heads to leave the tower and make the short journey, not more than five hundred metres, to the nearest of the six towers. This happened to be the Chinese tower where, on some occasions, despite the inter-tower discord, these unofficial visitors could find a welcome.

Night life was more lively in the Chinese tower then elsewhere. The music was more compelling, interesting and exciting. It was claimed they had a forest on the ground floor. The women sometimes put on a floor show. There were appetising morsels to eat, available for UU tokens, and a brand of surprisingly palatable wine.

Such visits met with official disapproval. A night-soil youth had slipped off to visit the Chinese tower, where it was said he had a lover. Two mornings later, his body was found naked and frozen in a rock fault. Although some diplomatic relations remained between the two towers, personal visits – unless of a formal nature – were prohibited.

Still, some people tried for a personal visit, but were nearly always detected by the re-entry tests seeing their air tanks were not depleted to the extent their length of absence would require. And then they were liable to meet Phipp's fist. Not only was he unfriendly, he was a keen pugilist.

So, he did enjoy his work. But there was, as he had mentioned to Noel, still a serious problem bugging him. His partness Sheea had borne him three children; that was back on Earth, before either of them had qualified for Mars. In Tharsis, they had quarrelled violently.

'You thought you could boss me about back in Nova Scotia,' she had said. 'It's a new life here. I will remain cordial to you, but you are no longer my bully and my boss. And you will never sleep with me again. Got that clear in your thick head?'

Phipp had got it clear. Being gate-keeper suited him. It gave him a reason to sleep away from Sheea.

But a year ago, Sheea had borne a child by another man. She had had another man in her bed, the bitch. He was glad the brat had died.

He had sworn he would kill the man who had dared to screw his woman. This he swore again when, as arranged, he had gone to consult Noel in her room.

She regarded him, now calm, from under her long lashes.

'You may or may not be aware of the terrestrial killings taking place, the West all but overcome by terrorism, while we can live here in perfect safety. Just to talk of killing affronts our Martian intentions. Don't you understand that?'

Phipp leant forward, fists clenched.

'Look,' he blustered. 'I rescued Sheea from the gutter. She had earned some wages, enough to go to university, but there she was, no job, all but starving. I looked after her. I had a little food-distribution racket—'

'You say you saved her from the gutter? Our records disagree. Her terrestrial family is well situated, her brother president of Harvard Business School. They are wealthy.' Noel tried not to call him a liar outright. 'What do you claim were your early experiences of Sheea then?'

'I'd had a whole lot of girls. They could not resist me. They like a strong man. Sheea was different. Looking back, I can't see what she was at.'

'You believe she was devious and somehow using you?'

He raised his head and let his jaw hang open.

'Look, I put up with her, OK? I can see you don't believe me, but

119

I did. Her brother was against me, always. We had three kids before we booked in for Mars.'

Noel sighed lightly. 'I see. And what about these kids?' Part of her duty was to let people talk privately. She did not relish conversations such as these, but tried not to be judgemental.

'We brought them with us, worse luck. Squirrel – he's the oldest – Daisie – we call her Daze – and little Piggy, who's, I dunno, about six.'

'Does Sheea look after them?'

'I look after the gate. That's a full-time job. Responsible.'

'Does Sheea look after them?'

'Well, she was pregnant, innit? If I could lay my hands on him that did it . . .'

'Let me advise you, Phipp. Control yourself. As we all have to do. It's our duty to put on a cheerful, calm appearance, whatever we're really feeling.'

23
The Four Birds

Noel was a neat person, her hair always tidy, her manner always cool. She took her own advice and controlled herself. Behind her decision to venture to Mars lay a sad history of an unloving mother and a marriage to a brutal man. Even on Tharsis, occupying an important position, she had never entirely forgotten the miseries of her early life. That made her more tolerant of the shortcomings of others.

All the same, she shrieked with anger when Piggy ran into her. Piggy was whizzing down the corridor on his bike and unable to stop in time.

'You're getting to be a big boy, Piggy. You must think of others.'

'Once I cycled right along the front at Blackpool. It's so boring here. Why can't we have birds, like they do in the Sud-Am tower? They have lots of birds there.'

'Well, Piggy dear, we only heard one bird, you know.'

'I saw more than that. Sitting in the background when that lady was talking. Looking a bit funny.'

She scrutinised his pale and honest face. 'Are you sure?'

'Course I'm sure or I wouldn't say it.' He stared back at her.

'Why didn't you say so at the time?'

He sniggered. 'Some stupid grown-up would have argued with me. You're always arguing. That's all there is to do in this dump.'

When she returned to her office, Noel got Yerat, her assistant, to play back the message from Sud-Am. What she saw persuaded her to summon Dr Nivec to her side. Noel knew that before Nivec had qualified as a doctor, he had once served as an aviarist in the San Diego Zoo. Back then he'd had a head of red hair, but the years had bleached it whilst causing his shoulders to stoop.

She played him the Sud-Am clip.

'Of course, our attention was focused on that lady talking about religion. Not only were we quite shocked,' Nivec said, 'but the young lady was very attractive.' He gave Noel a sidelong look, but she made no response.

'What are these things in the background?'

He studied them. 'Yes, there are – I've counted them – four birds visible. All are very still and three of them, at least, are diseased. You see how their eyes are crusted over. This one on the left is the worst affected.'

Nivec pointed at it. 'The poor creature's eyes are swollen shut.'

'Under the UU agreement, birds and other pets are forbidden – for obvious reasons. Food shortage for one thing. And hygiene.'

'Yes, but these birds could easily have been smuggled in. These we can see here will soon be dead. They are suffering from – well, most likely, House Finch disease, or possibly Avian pox. It's hard to tell without a proper diagnosis. What do you propose to do about it?'

Noel said firmly that there was nothing they could legally do.

When Nivec, rather reluctantly, left her presence, Noel messaged Mangalian at UU. 'Keeping of pets was disallowed. Birds unlikely to thrive in interior environment. Tower may contain other pets. Also inhabitants have reverted to religion. Should we intervene or do nothing? Will you address tower in question? Noel.'

This remote communication felt acutely insufficient. She deeply missed Mangalian and sometimes even fantasised about him. He was the one man she had ever loved. And he, of course, was millions of miles away.

There had been discussion about how Phipp's breach with the Chinese should be finally put to rest. Diplomacy was suffering. There was always the possibility that West tower might run out of food if a UU shipment was delayed, in which case someone would have to go begging to the nearest tower. Meaning the Chinese tower.

A delegation of three was selected to go and eat humble pie.

Tad was appointed leader, since he had a few words of Mandarin at his command. Tad was glad to undertake the task. He had failed to make a mark so far in the West tower community, and he liked the Chinese and was eager to contribute to the company of which he formed part.

He cleaned himself up and went with two companions to make some amends for the violent attack on their visitor and the much belated apology.

A large slab like a giant's tombstone stood to one side of the China tower gate. It was headed by a decorative dragon, below which was an elaborate inscription of some kind.

They were admitted without delay. Removing their face-masks, they found that the scent of the tower differed from their own. The space was hung about with saffron-coloured drapes from floor almost to ceiling. Just below the ceiling a balcony ran; on the balcony were men, standing still, watching for possible intruders, somewhat spoiling the otherwise welcoming effect of the decor.

An early surprise came when a lackey led the trio through a small forest. They heard birdsong. The trees, their bark, their leaves, seemed at first to be real. Authentic though they appeared, they proved to be formed from a variety of plastics, and the birdsong was artificial.

The lackey escorted them to a small inner chamber in which stood a table bearing a simple meal, with ruby-coloured liquid in glasses. The room was in semi-darkness, lit only by a small electric lamp placed in the middle of the table. 'Bit frugal with light,' one of the three said in an undertone.

The trio stood there rather awkwardly until the lackey motioned them to sit and eat. They sat but did not eat, Tad appreciating the ambience, the other two suffering slightly from culture shock.

Music sounded soothingly, played mainly on what sounded like two pi pas. Music of stillness, of reticence . . .

Another lackey entered, more grandly dressed than the earlier man. He beckoned them wordlessly to follow him. Tad's feelings were overwhelmed by the music, which brought back in a flood memories of the past, of his days in the embassy in Beijing, long before he'd settled down with Ida.

The visitors were shown into a small room, quite luxuriously furnished, but again low-lit. There they were required to stand. A gong sounded and a woman entered by a door behind them. She was enrobed and her long dark hair was tied by a purple ribbon so as to fall over her left shoulder. Her eyelashes were long, her lips red. Her beautiful oval face was unpainted.

She folded her hands in her lap and studied her visitors without speaking. The attendant said, 'Here to greet you is Chang Mu Gongcha.'

Tad and his companions bowed, uncertain what to do next.

Chang Mu Gongcha spoke in almost unaccented English. She greeted Tad and the others courteously, adding that she would be pleased to have closer contact with the West tower 'peacefully, of course.'

When asked how many personnel there were in the tower, Chang Mu Gongcha named a low number, 'fewer than one hundred.' She added, 'You will notice we mostly select only light-weight women to journey here. That cuts journey time and ensures better health on arrival.'

Chang Mu Gongcha asked if they would like something to eat or, alternatively, to inspect the art room. She had an hour to spare before a meeting she must attend.

Tad opted for the art room, while the other two were escorted away – to finish the food they had been offered earlier.

For Tad, it was a delight to be alone with Chang Mu Gongcha. He asked what was inscribed on the great plaque before the entrance to the tower.

The answer was, a quotation from the analects of Confucius:

'Tzu-hsia said "Even minor arts are sure to have their worthwhile aspects, but the gentleman does not take them up because the fear of a man who would go a long way is that he should be bogged down.'"

The art room was full of strange artefacts, some carved from resin, some formed from fabric, some painted on the walls.

Tad admitted to being greatly impressed. 'We have no art,' he said. 'Not really, in our tower.'

Chang Mu Gongcha's response was a careless remark to the effect that art kept people busy.

'More than that, surely. Back home, much art was held in high esteem.'

She looked askance at him, a half-smile on her face, then changed the subject. 'Earlier, you complimented me on my English. But I had a good opportunity to learn. In the University of Chengdu I was head of the – well, it translates as the Department of Great Passed-Away People.'

'The Illustrious Dead?'

'Yes, but we are careful with that particular last word you used. It was my fortune to be delegated to represent my university at the negotiations leading to the establishment of the UU. So, there in Chicago I saw a real living city. It's true the city was then breaking up with rioting but for most people life went on pretty much as normal.'

He reminded her that Chicago had been destroyed.

'It was after I left, luckily,' Gongcha said with a light laugh. 'You see I was then avid for the UU and the Mars adventure.'

'As was I! It broke up my relationship with my partness. She preferred to become a bank manager.'

They looked at each other, seriously at first. Then both burst into laughter.

Gongcha said, 'Maybe she finds more adventure in the bank than there is here . . .' Eyes then downcast, she said quietly, 'This was to be the great human adventure, wasn't it? And yet . . .' She did not complete the sentence.

He felt his heart beating faster. 'It's constricting, isn't it?'

Her lips parted, revealing white teeth. 'Perhaps we need some adventure . . .' The words sounded to him as honey would sound, had it a tongue.

'Supposing we started a joint art class . . . We might then find it had its uses.'

With her words, 'I am sure we would work compatibly together,' she laid a hand on his arm.

He covered her hand with his.

Trudging back through the tawny sand of Tharsis, Tad found his mind and body in a storm of sensations, reverential and libidinous, brutish and high-flown. Her fragrance still lingered in his senses, and he imagined her naked before him. The destitution of the land around him was transformed into a riot of luxuria . . .

As was his mind, where he found himself submerged into her bodily being. Chang Mu Gongcha . . . the beauty of her name, like the sound of a pi pa or the resonance of a ruan, that stringed instrument, so sweet when plucked.

24
Consolations of Knowledge and Sex

At the next meeting of the West, as soon as the Brightener opened, Tad raised the subject of organising an art class. Much muttering followed. Yerat, who had been Barrin's lover, spoke up. 'We don't have any spare material from which to create art.'

'The Chinese use whatever is spare and handy,' said Tad. 'A wooden plank can be transformed into a kind of spirit.'

'The Chinese may need art,' said a pregnant woman called Blior. 'In my opinion we don't. Or rather, are we not already practising art, living here in close quarters and that without quarrelling? That seems to me like an art form, already being practised.'

'No, no,' said Tad. 'That is simply natural behaviour. We are polite, circumspect, simply to make this great experiment work.

'Art is surely something different, a pretence of some kind – a story, let's say, to take it at its simplest – which reminds us of a deeper sense which we might not otherwise acknowledge.'

Squirrel spoke. 'Sorry, but I think Tad is sort of right. For instance, we could put on a play. I wouldn't mind putting on a play. In fact, I think I could write one. I would want to be in it.'

Various voices voted that the youngster should be encouraged to do as he suggested. Squirrel blushed red at this acceptance.

A woman called Deim who worked with Noel said that she thought they should move to more serious matters.

'Art is a serious matter,' said Tad, indignantly.

Ignoring this remark, Deim reported that the Battle of Five States, so-called, continued back on Earth. So far, Tharsis had taken little notice of it; after all, armed struggle was taking place everywhere. Armed struggle was one of the reasons why they were on Mars, for security and for the possible expansion of wisdom.

The news from so many parts of Earth continued to be bad. It was a year or so ago that the armed forces of Russo-Musil had invaded and taken over Greenland. In a troubled world this had largely been ignored. The US President had complained strongly, but American forces were engaged in the Middle East and in parts of Indonesia.

Russo-Musil Greenland had only remained for a year. Then had come the invasion launched against Newfoundland, which had been overcome with comparative ease. Negotiations were taking place when another strike was launched against the state of Maine. Maine was overcome.

The US President resigned. A military clique took over, calling back air support from Java. Another Russo-Musil advance using extensive field nukes gained the enemy most of New Hampshire. Their success won them support from West Russia, the state known as Belominsk after the great lands of Russia had broken into four separate states.

With a fierce push, much of the coastline had been taken before US forces, supported by troops from Holland and Britain, formed a defensive line. This halted the enemy drive southward. But the city of Portland was virtually destroyed by nuclear attack.

The destruction had encompassed the University of Portland – a member of the UU. A small proportion of the finances supporting the West tower had therefore been lost.

This unhappy news quelled all discussion of art.

VIOLENT STORM WRECKS PHILIPPINES
MANILA CITY FLOODED WAIST DEEP
HUNDREDS BELIEVED DROWNED

Daark was coming off shift and having what passed for a coffee in the canteen, when Iggog entered. Daark gave a nod which encouraged Iggog to join him.

'How's the living universe?' Iggog's jocular enquiry was intended merely as a sort of joke.

'The newly discovered normon contains amino acid, otherwise nothing biological, though there is a group linkage similar to linkages we find in DNA. Normons seem particularly prevalent in orbits about Mars, which implies –'

'Hang on!' Iggog said. 'I can't take all this stuff in!' She began to paint her lips.

'You asked me, so I'm telling you. Try to learn. The frequency of normons hereabouts suggests that something like DNA was on its way to a transformation similar to DNA, although by no means the same, when a catastrophe of some kind struck Mars, thus decreasing the possibilities for life to develop. The normons may yet coalesce. So that the universe – the local section at least – may then be considered "alive".'

Daark sat back and regarded Iggog for a response.

'I'm sure you're right,' said Iggog, scratching her nose.

They settled down to discuss the latest news. Phipp had made a pass at a woman returning on her own from the Chinese tower – Phipp who had already caused trouble. The woman had, according to Troed who had been nearby, given Phipp a 'healthy belt in the mush', to use Troed's words.

'But the funniest thing,' said Iggog, who always seemed to know what others did not, 'is that the mush-belter was Ooma. Ooma! I suppose you know that she used to be a guy? Changed her sex.'

Daark confessed he did not know.

'Yes, she was a guy called Tompkins until she had a sex-change op.'

Daark felt bound to ask the obvious question: 'How do you know all this?'

'He was riff-raff. So was I, but I was in the police,' said Iggog. 'I did not much like being a cop, but it gave you the chance to see how others lived.

'Do you remember when we were preparing to board the *Confu* we had a series of lectures from a guy called Morgan Something? Remember his T-shirt, "Different Shit"? He knew about that sex-change. He once had a dig at "Tompkins" . . .'

It was not that Daark enjoyed this conversation, nor did he enjoy revealing his ignorance to this gossipy lady, but his curiosity was roused.

'He – she – must be an unstable character.' Iggog pulled a wry face. 'How come the UU okayed Ooma for the trip? Weren't we supposed to be the crème de la crème?'

Iggog permitted herself one of her sly triumphant smiles.

'Well . . . look, the famous Mangalian was duped. Does that surprise you? Sure, a ton of dough was forthcoming, but was used – or some of it – to bribe the interviewers. "Let a few trouble-makers in," they said. Which means, "Get 'em off the planet." They had to. Bad as things were back home, the really clever, the wise, the scholarly, had too much sense to go for the exile enterprise. They had to fill up the quota with scum like me!'

Daark gave a short laugh.

'You didn't realise that?'

'I'm not sure I believe it now.'

Iggog leant across the table. 'Take the best of them, Noel – or Rosemary Cavendish, as she used to be. I heard a rumour that Mangalian was married to the daughter of no less than Earth President Ban Mu Kai's daughter. But he was also having it off with Rosemary, who worked in his offices. He saw his secret was going to get out, to be leaked. Always money to be made out of scandal . . . So Mangalian went to Kai and made a clean breast of it.

'So then Kai saw to it that Rosemary was shipped out . . .'

'You're kidding me. That can't be true!' Daark felt his anger rising at this fanciful gossip. He drained his coffee carton.

Iggog made a face. 'It's corruption, isn't it? Gets everywhere, like dry rot. You can believe me or not as you please. But I'll tell you one more thing. Once Kai learned that Mangalian was not to be trusted and that as a youth he had been what you might call a "rake"– Kai wasn't going to allow the offence to go unpunished.

He sent in a heavy or two and they carved Mangalian up. His body has never been found – not that anyone was encouraged to look very hard.'

Daark thought, *Surely even here we'd know if Mangalian was dead?* But all he said was that he did not know what to say.

'You could say it's lousy coffee,' Iggog suggested. She giggled girlishly.

As relations became cordial once more, a group of amateur historians drawn from all six towers began to meet once a month. They called themselves Thistorians, to acknowledge a certain divorce from events back on Earth which did not directly concern the post-Curiosity planet, Mars. This month they were looking at the UU, and how 'knowledge' had been so significant in the Mars enterprise. The UU's step into the unknown – or at least into the only partly known – had been in the name of knowledge and human advancement. Of course, there had been much debate on the precise definitions of 'knowledge' and 'human advancement'.

It had been decided:

a) That the Big K, as knowledge and advancement were called colloquially, was an integral part of the intelligence which constituted a major role in human consciousness.

b) There were types of Big K which served only a minor part of intelligence, such as knowing of which country Tirana was the capital, or who was the oldest man/woman on Earth, or who was the most famous golf player in the world. All such items became known as 'boot-locker knowledge' or 'quiz-answer quotes'.

c) 'Knowing how' and 'knowing when' were essential components of Big K – such as knowing when and how a journey to Mars became possible, so that knowledge could be exercised and (most likely) enlarged.

d) "Pure K" is a suspect term, since research may reveal senses and areas of reason hitherto unknown. 'Abstract K' is also suspect, since there is already an aspect in which Big K is all abstract.

e) Big K in part requires organisation, such as universities provide, whereby elements of the past may be transposed to the future,

often to create new futures (in areas such as government, speculation, and affirmative pleasure). It is agreed, however, that solitary
geniuses may advance knowledge, often in remarkable ways.[4]

f) Thus 'the unknown' as a subject of investigation is an essential
    part of Big K.
g) The definition of Big K was drawn up. The universities could
    move on to more taxing matters.

Thus, to some jokers, the innate compromises resulting in
deformed and unsound conclusions about knowledge were paralleled
by the deformed babies born later on the Red Planet.

As the Thistorians recorded, from the findings of the two hydrologists, a surprisingly short time had elapsed before the shipping of
humans in sizeable numbers across millions of miles of the raging
element still known as 'space'. The towers had been set up and partially
occupied almost immediately and were stocked with bioscientifically
passed provisions.

Many marvelled that this great challenge had been seized upon
in the first place, let alone achieved so quickly . . .

Here and there, even in this desperate period when the planet Earth
was sinking under the weight of over-population and underhand
warfare, there were a few scholars who recalled the words of a long-
dead Scottish poet: 'The best laid schemes o' mice an' men gang aft
agley.'

It was the enforced economies and abridgements – the distances
– the great agley-ment of existence – which followed that caused Sheea
to sleep in a dormitory full of women instead of a little room of her
own, but nevertheless to permit a lover to creep into her inviting bed.

Women slept here in their own beds, each bed curtained off from
the next. Separate cabins were still to be constructed; material had
to be imported. These temporary dormitories filled the top floors
but one of each of the towers.

---

[4] Here were instanced geniuses such as Akhenaten, Charles Darwin, Konstantin
Tsiolkovsky, Albert Einstein and others.

Above these dormitories, accessible only by a non-stop elevator from the ground floor, was the Astronomy Department with its various telescopes, cameras and computers and other paraphernalia, where, in the West tower, the planet Xeno was the particular subject of intensive study.

Of a night, all above was activity. Shutters were open. On the floor below, Sheea and her like had their eyes closed in restful slumbers. Or perhaps an enterprising lover had negotiated with the guard at the door and crept into a wakeful and welcoming bed. As had happened in Sheea's case – a small and furtive arrangement, but the entire known universe would be told of its results.

Nor had her murmurs of delight originated as solo music. Other instruments were being played in various parts of the dormitory, and the guardian at the door was accumulating pockets full of tokens.

Not all terrestrial pleasures were easily shed.

25
Meeting an Astronomer

Daze and Piggy found plenty to occupy them. They slept in hammocks which could serve as spaceships or submarines or the trees they dimly remembered. They had inflatable coloured balls and an electronic bug which whizzed about on one wall, defying attempts to zap it.

Sometimes they teased Thirn, because she was shy and looked miserable. 'You know we're really on Saturn,' they said.

'Please go away,' Thirn said. 'I'm not in the mood for this. My brother's fighting in Peshawar.'

'Pooh! There's no such planet!'

Only recently had Squirrel, fifteen years of age, withdrawn from this juvenile gaiety. He could be seen lingering in the corridors, enduring the effects of puberty and testosterone.

Wandering into the canteen, which served also as a bank, he sat over a mug of coffee, blank-faced, not drinking. His sister Daze peeped round the door, pulled a funny face at him, and disappeared.

'You all right?' Yerat, the waitress, asked Squirrel.

'Why shouldn't I be?'

She pulled a face not unlike Daze's. 'Dozens of reasons,' she said, moving away.

This exchange was watched by the Banker/Canteen Supervisor, by name Stroy. Stroy was a warm-hearted woman, forever restless, plump and pleasing to the eye, forever smiling.

She in her turn went over to Squirrel. 'Are you bored, lad? How can you ever be bored when the library houses all the world's books, from Plato onwards?'

'Plato!' He echoed the name contemptuously.

'It's just an example. But you'd find stuff in Plato to surprise you.'

He made no answer. She retreated, dismissing the adolescent from her mind. She had been about to make a manoeuvre of her own. A tray of food had been prepared for the Astronomy floor. A waitress usually took it up. Stroy wanted a look at the top floor and had decided to carry up the tray herself.

The non-stop elevator delivered her. Blinds rendered the quarters in deep shade. Over in one corner, three people were sleeping in stacked bunks. Stroy had forgotten that astronomers were most busy at night.

When Stroy stepped into the observatory, a man long in years, with white hair to match, came forward and took the tray from her. Smiling, he said in a gentle voice, 'I don't think we have seen you before.' When he smiled, she registered his bright blue eyes shining in a pale unhealthy countenance. Her impression was that she stood in the presence of an unusual personality.

'I haven't been here before. Haven't dared to. My name's Stroy.'

'I see. Somewhat like Helen of Stroy.'

'Not quite, I have to say. I regret the food is so sparse. Supplies are running low. We'll have to go on to half-rations until the next UU drone arrives.'

'It doesn't matter.' He cleared his throat. He shook his long white locks, just enough to make them tremble. 'Philosophy teaches us that the flesh is less important than we like to believe. I am certainly in need of that perception – though of its truth I am not fully convinced.'

'So. What do you do up here, if I may ask? Are you studying the Massive Solar Companion – Nemesis?'

'Oh, that's rather gone out of fashion, I fear.'

'You mean you haven't got the telescopes to do a search – to find a new body like it?'

Chuckling, he said. 'Not new – ages old. No mention in the Koran or Bible, though. "God made the stars" . . . it's just a wild guess.' He shook his head reprovingly. 'Well, we all like to believe in something, however absurd . . . The more ancient the better.'

'People didn't know any better in the old days,' Stroy said in a tone suggesting she agreed with every word he said.

He peered at her. 'I cannot say which I most deplore, those who did not know any way of knowing better, or those who, when the better is already known, don't bother to learn.'

She said, 'Oh, it must be those latter people.'

'Then you have resolved that problem for me,' he replied in a gently mocking tone. 'But as for Nemesis, we do not have a telescope strong enough in existence here.'

'You need more astronomers on the board back on Earth.'

'But they may be our rivals,' he said, turning to inspect vaguely the tray Stroy had brought.

'The gods – not to mention the salaries – must have got in the way. Although our 'scope is a present from NASA, it isn't powerful enough to sight Nemesis from Tharsis. So I stick to – well, to Eris . . . 'This tray is my one solace.'

He raised a hand and waggled an admonitory finger.

'But we are not idle, young lady. The UU keep us hard at work.' His manner changed abruptly. 'But I should be polite and introduce myself. My name is Ficht. How d'y'do? Wie geht? In my native Germany, I was a professor, but on Tharsis we have rightly abandoned titles. I was born in the Duchy of Wurtzberg. I had an elder brother; we were never close. My father was a wealthy lawyer, remote from the two of us. My mother died when I was very young, from a vene-real disease. Thus was my character shaped. Mis-shaped, I should say.' He cleared his throat again. 'Will you tell me of your upbringing? Is it amusing or tragic in any way?'

Those blue eyes were fixed on her as if, she thought, he wanted to eat her. Feeling more than slightly uneasy, she responded, 'I was brought up in a pleasant country town, Hampden Ferrers, in

Wiltshire, sir. Or it was pleasant until a biscuit factory opened. It employed foreign labour, and then trouble began. And so on . . .'

Apparently with a touch of contempt, Ficht said, 'You had parents, I assume.'

'My parents and my step-father were pretty affluent. They had emigrated from Bavaria. They sent me to Keble College in Oxford.'

'Why did they emigrate? Was it something sexual?'

Ignoring the question, she told him, 'While I was away, my parents were attacked one night and our house burnt down. My father died. My mother re-married almost at once.'

She wondered why she had told him so much.

Ficht seemed indifferent to her story, asking merely, 'And had you culture? Cultivation? Was Oxford good for you?'

'Yes, I think so. I took a particular interest in the paintings of Holman Hunt. Later, I wrote a book on him.'

'But culturally? Pardon, but this Holman Hunt doesn't amount to much. The spirit – if one may use the expression – the spirit of mankind, the flame – is missing. The unity of all sciences, the disunity of mankind. What marks our anomalous existence within a great inorganic world?'

'I would find all that stuff pretty pretentious. But, well, I mean, in the life of Holman Hunt one finds the struggle – well, just to be oneself and to create. Create as best one can . . .'

He turned away. His shoulder blades showed through his thin jacket.

He cleared his throat, turning back

'I am attracted by your youth and vitality, so I endeavour to impress you. My apologies, dear lady. You asked me what we do here. Come, I will show you.'

He went to one of the telescopes. Stroy followed.

They looked not through the telescope but rather at a screen below, where the incoming image was being stored.

A brownish image glowed, speckled with miniature bodies, some smoothly round, most of them irregularly shaped. And something grander: a globe as if lit from its interior. Its otherwise barren surface was seemingly stained here and there.

'That, my dear, is 2003 UB313. The jewel-like UB313.'

Ficht had spoken of his life in steady tones. Now his voice trembled with emotion. His somewhat immobile expression had broken into an involuntary smile of delight. 'See? The wonderful unknown. Unknowable.'

He cleared his throat.

Without thinking what she was doing, Stroy put a compassionate arm about him. She felt his slight start; otherwise he gave no indication that she had touched him.

'UB313 . . . It's known as Eris, once called Xena. Have you heard of it?'

'It's in the Kuiper Belt, isn't it?'

He straightened up. Making a circular gesture with one hand, he said, 'You realise that our whole insignificant little solar system is enclosed within a so-called Oort Cloud containing billions of bodies, comets and such like, incoherent matter. Most people do not know or care about the Oort Cloud. Their psychology of life is therefore warped and their understanding incomplete.'

She did not comprehend this latter statement. Nor did she scoff at it. She was aware there was much she did not understand.

'Perhaps our lives are too small and harried to . . .' He put one of his frail hands out as if to have it clutched. 'I feel your intelligence, Stroy. And indeed your modesty. How I wish you and I could be closer and I could teach you like a daughter.' He added, 'But always I have to withdraw.' He paused, looking away from her to add, 'From any human contact . . .'

Again he cleared his throat.

She detected a conflict in the wish Ficht expressed and sensed a veiled eroticism. She moved away from him, and possibly from her own ambiguity. An inner prompting told her she did not like Ficht.

'You should take some exercise for your health's sake. You could have a short walk with me, just round the tower, say? If you wish.'

'I haven't left this room once in the past year. I'm content, I suppose.' Possibly he sensed her condescension.

'You might enjoy it outside.'

Even as she spoke, urging him, a new compound word came to her: selbsthilfloszwang. Oh yes, she thought, helpless self-compulsion. She had often experienced it. Indeed, with that absurd compound word, she had forced herself to apply for the Mars trip – in the main to escape her ponderous Bavarian parents, particularly her step-father. It was a Tharsis word, maybe.

She forced it from consciousness to escort Ficht into the elevator.

When they reached the outer door, the gatekeeper, Phipp, was having a violent row with a smaller man, an Exwo, calling him vile names and shouting him down whenever he tried to explain something.

Phipp's elder son, Squirrel, was nearby. 'I bet you did it!' he shouted. 'Exwos were always going to be trouble.'

Red-faced, Phipp shouted, 'You see, even the kid knows! Clear off! I'll beat you up if I set eyes on you again!'

The man slunk off, with Squirrel following at a distance. Phipp's demeanour changed immediately, as he turned to Stroy and Ficht.

'Excuse me. Sorry to keep you waiting. Please come through here.'

'You seemed a good deal upset,' said Stroy, unable to resist the jibe.

'I got much to be upset about,' said Phipp. 'I'm down here on duty, my partness is up the top, so this sneak gets at her, the bastick. He has her. Sticks it up her . . . Now she's given birth – like she's sending me a message – and you can see what that means.'

'It's nothing to do with us,' said Ficht to Stroy, as they passed into the open. In the air, the dusk, the low oxygen levels. Earth not to be seen.

They had hardly taken a dozen steps when Ficht clasped Stroy's hand and stood still. He muttered half to himself. 'Violent man! Vile man! Yes, vile and violent . . . How could he be so sure the other fellow had impregnated his wife? Partness, I mean.'

'The son thought so too.' She saw that the incident had somehow excited the astronomer.

'Maybe they enjoyed imagining such a thing happening . . .'

Faint sunlight filtered in long horizontal strokes between the two nearer towers, the Sud-Am and Chinese. Stroy considered it a beautiful scene, silent, resembling a stage set in a play she had watched in her youth on Earth. A line of an old poem drifted into her thoughts –

. . . a violet in the dewy prime of nature

not – what exactly? – not permanent or lasting?

Well, it had been long ago and she was never likely to see a violet again.

Ficht was unmoved. He stood staring down at the trodden regolith. He muttered something about agoraphobia. Then, 'Starlight seduction, the suction . . .'

'Come on, Ficht! You are used to staring across light years. How can this little strip of land upset you?' Stroy took a firm hold on his stick-like upper arm to move him along.

'No, no, I need to return, Stroy. You don't understand. I'm just nothing – non-participant. Why should you . . . order me about?'

She thought how like a child he was.

'Please take me back in. I want to show you something.'

'Oh, for crying out loud . . .' *Selbsthilfloszwang.*

Trying not to lose patience, she guided Ficht back through the gate. Daze was playing there by her father, Phipp. She ran up and inspected the pair closely, looking intently at Ficht.

'Doesn't he like it on Mars?' she asked.

Glancing at her watch, Stroy saw it was time she was back on duty. But first she was determined to get Ficht to the hospital. She manoeuvred him into the special ward elevator.

He stared fixedly at her. 'I would like to copulate with you, Stroy. Even at my late age, I have never yet copulated in my whole life. Not once. I try to imagine what it would be like. Do you enjoy it, may I ask?'

She was taken aback, both amused and angered. 'Is that supposed to be some kind of a proposal? You must see what they have to say about it in the ward. If they believe you, maybe they'd fix you up with a dutiful nurse.'

'No, no, you don't understand. It's my lebensangst . . .'

Oh, hurry up and get there, she thought, knowing that this lift, often carrying wounded, was geared to a slow ascent.

'You see I have never in my life managed to achieve an erection.' He spoke reflectively, fixing his gaze on Stroy's face. He cleared his throat. 'Don't you find that curious? All I possess is a long flaccid pipe of flesh for the passage of urine. My regret is that I can never copulate with an adorable creature such as you. Shall I show you it?'

'Sorry, we're here now, Ficht.' The elevator stopped and the door slid open.

She handed Ficht over to the charge nurse. He must have realised this was by way of a final parting with Stroy. He said nothing. Tears fell like drops of mercury from his eyes as he was led away.

Stroy went behind a screen, sat down on a chair and cried considerably.

The matron in charge of the overall running of the hospital day-by-day, Herrit, was comparatively new on Tharsis. She had arrived by the most recent manned ship. Even with the lighter Martian gravity, she needed support at first, since the journey had weakened her heart; it pumped more slowly, leaving her faint and gasping. Only under the carefully graded routine exercises, supervised by a cardiologist, was her health returning. She took charge of Ficht. Now she was in the position of being able to nurse others more seriously damaged than she had been.

Herrit saw Stroy crying. She did not interfere. There was weeping enough in the hospital beds.

The general cleaner was making his rounds. He arrived at the hospital with his ride-on vacuum-scourer, and greeted Herrit with a smile. 'How's that heart of yours today, Herrit? Feeling any better?'

'All the better for seeing you, Rasir, dear.'

Rasir's skin shone like ebony. He was lightly built. His head was shaved. He had a sullen expression except when he smiled, but he generally smiled, as now, since he had taken a particular liking to Herrit.

She asked, in a teasing way, 'Are you still sleeping up in the Astronomy?'

'Well, I like to be close to the stars. And I don't snore. So they put up with me.' The brilliant smile flashed on.

Herrit tried not to imagine what it might be like to be in bed with him. 'Have you found any dragon-flies up there?'

Rasir shook his head. 'We seem to be on the wrong part of Mars for dragon-flies.'

Mention of dragon-flies was a grim joke, they had between them.

Back on Earth, in Africa – this was the story Rasir had told Herrit when she had first arrived on Tharsis and was feeling low – he lived with his family in a village on the banks of the river Kasai, only three days' walk to Kinshasa. There were a lot of problems and some elements of the family had become separate. They called themselves Freedom Fighters and had been given a gun of sorts and a meal now and then.

'How can you have Freedom if you become a Fighter? It is a deception. Freedom comes only with peace.' So said Rasir's wise old dad, whose brother had joined this bad army. He said it every morning when he got up and went to piss in the river. Of course Rasir was not called Rasir in those days, nor had he any aspirations, though he did regard his father as holy.

One day, he was told by his mother to go to Kinshasa to get some medicine for his father's throat, which was hurting him.

On the way, Rasir was walking through what was left of the forest when he encountered some Freedom Fighters. And there, to his delight, he saw his uncle, now calling himself Binja La Shithole (pronounced Shi-Toley). Rasir ran towards him, arms wide, calling him by the family name.

Binja also advanced.

When Rasir was up close, his uncle landed a savage blow on the boy's face.

Rasir fell unconscious. He lay sprawling in the dust. When he awoke, there was no one to be seen. But on his arm outstretched in the dirt a dragon-fly had settled. Its body was of a diaphanous blue, finer, purer, than any gown woman ever wore. Its wings held the thinnest veins of gold, which fluttered gently all the while. Its eyes were little green balls which peered ahead.

Many such insects had Rasir seen before, but never so close or so available for study. At Rasir's slight movement, the dragon-fly took to its wings. It circled above his head and then was away, making for the river. He watched until he could see it no longer.

What he told Herrit was that this beautiful creature had been a spirit messenger. It had awakened him to the fact that somewhere there was a place where poverty and ignorance did not exist and members of a family did not attack one another.

He got up to make for Kinshasa. And work. And study. His nose was still bleeding.

Food rations were getting smaller, but they had no worries about water shortages; or rather, they had not thought to worry about its running out: soundings had shown that the cavern containing the subterranean water was vast.

No complaints then until the water became a little cloudy. Anxieties were aroused that possibly they had drained an underground river, now drying up. After some discussion, it was agreed that a volunteer should go down into the great subterranean cave and report on the state of affairs.

Thirn, the woman who had run a shop by the sea, volunteered to investigate. She had frequently, in her more youthful days, swum in the sea at night.

'No, I should go,' Squirrel said quietly to Thirn. 'Everyone thinks I'm bad – I want to show them I am not bad.'

She regarded him coldly. 'But you had sex with your mother, didn't you? Don't deny it – she told me. I'll keep it confidential – but for her, not for you.'

'She needed it as much as me.'

Unmoved, she said, 'Sorry, Squirrel, I got my needs too, so shut it.'

26

Life on Mars! The Capture of Things

The pale daylight lit a number of people coming from the Western tower.

A hole had been excavated in rough and broken territory some distance from the tower. Two guards stood by it. Thirn came and stood shivering beside them.

'Don't worry, old pet,' said one guard reassuringly. 'There's nothing to harm you down there.'

'I'll see about that,' she replied. 'Fool that I am for volunteering.'

A crowd had gathered to see Thirn being lowered down into the depths. They were uneasy, but anything happening on a dead world ranked as an Event. Some people clapped as Thirn was lowered into the hole. A silence fell. Almost immediately there came from this intrepid woman a cry like a reverberating belch, magnified by the hollow chamber. It was followed by a shriek to be hauled up. As soon as her head emerged above ground, a head seemingly bodiless, Thirn cried out – not from cowardice but out of need for a net.

'Things!' she cried. 'A net! Quick! There's something big down here!'

Such was the urgency of her tone it compelled people to start running about in that high-kneed Martian way. Until as if by magic – magic prohibited on Mars – a net was produced.

Thirn grabbed the net and commanded to be lowered again into the depths. Her head disappeared from the watchers' sight.

Everyone waited. What for? For life? The crowd fell into an anxious silence, the lonelinesses of the planet seemed to close in about them.

Shrieks and splashes magnified by the hollow of the cavern were as sounds issuing from a great throat. Then a perfectly clear cry of triumph, 'Got you, you bastick!'

'Are you okay?' shouted those clasping the rope above ground.

'Haul up! Haul like mad . . .' came the bellow.

They hauled. What appeared first was a largish lizard-like thing, struggling furiously in the net. Or was it two lizard-like things?

Yes, two of them – and followed by Thirn, heaving herself from the hole, gasping, shaking herself like an old dog. A towel was thrown round her. A guard gave her a breathing mask. She shook the towel about her ample shoulders, growling about the cold.

Attention switched immediately to the two struggling things. Little scientific curiosity here – not in the face of something to eat. The creatures were dragged back into the tower – straight to the kitchen. Pushing her way through the excited mob of people came Noel, cucumber-cool.

'I forbid you to kill these creatures. Science must come first. Get out of the way!'

'But they are real food,' Stroy protested.

Noel looked as if she was about to attack Stroy. 'Food! You must be mad. Can't you understand? Get a grip of yourself. We have found life on Mars! Life on Mars! Not just micro-organisms. Bodily life on Mars! This is our saving, do you realise?'

The crowd fell back before her.

'I found them, don't forget, Noel,' said Thirn, still wrapped in her towel.

'Correct, madam,' said Nivec, addressing Noel. 'Thank you. Life on Mars! This discovery will justify UU in the eyes of the world. We just need to find what category of beasts we have here. Nothing very pleasant, by the looks of them.'

146

'Yes, not "it" – but so much better – "them"! Stroy, shut these creatures into a container and take them immediately to the science rooms.'

So said Noel, and her order was obeyed. She clutched Nivec's arm. 'Wonderful!', she exclaimed. 'Wonderful! – And you too, Thirn, you're wonderful.'

'I'd say we're all wonderful,' said Nivec. 'Or will be when Earth gets our news . . .'

Thirn, now dressed in her usual overalls, sat on a chair in the corner of the lab. She wore a circle of stiff paper on which she had written 'I DISCOVERED LIFE ON MARS'. Because of her new status, she was allowed into the science rooms.

The creatures she had captured lay on the bench in transparent water-filled plastic tanks. They were unmoving until they would suddenly rise up and scratch in a fruitless endeavour to escape from their prison. They possessed long bony heads. Their eyes were large and milky – 'Like poached eggs,' Cood muttered. Their four legs were flat and fin-like, held close to the scaly body. They measured not more than two feet long.

Their bodies tapered into a stumpy tail. At their maximum, these bodies were not more than four inches wide and six deep. They were covered with something resembling scales, shiny and black, showing green in certain lights. When one of these creatures was turned over, its belly showed smooth and hard and of a pale white.

When they snarled, sharp curved front teeth showed. Behind these fangs lay only two pointed teeth on either side of a grey mouth.

'They are quiet and seem to be breathing easily in air,' said Cood. 'But I suspect that it's been just a few generations since they were only fish, do you agree?'

Nivec asked Thirn if she had caught them swimming.

'There were others of these same critters attacking them, or chasing all round, till I appeared,' said Thirn. 'A ridge of rock comes above water level down there. These two brutes were resting on top of the rock, out of the water.'

'So, a different species from the ones you saw in the water?'

'I can't say about that. It was dark and they were gone quickly. There's a tunnel leading from the main chamber and they were off down it in a flash.

'These two I caught, I thought they were a bit tired. Breathing air – there's oxygen underground, to some extent.'

'Thank you. Your account was very clear, Thirn,' said Nivec.

'Of course it was clear. I'm not a fool.'

Thirn's discovery had evidently banished her former shyness.

Cood said, 'We've got hold of a bit of history. History? Prehistory, I should say. Radiometric dating determines the end of the Permian Age as about 252 million years ago. We're talking Earth times here, of course.

'The Permian suffered a serious catastrophe. Some thing or things hit us – hit the Earth – and it took several million years for a biomass to recover. But out of that big black pit crawled –'

'Hang on,' Nivec interrupted, placing a retaining hand on Cood's arm. 'Look, we must talk about this before an assemblage of the whole tower – and link up with the other towers. Everyone here on Tharsis has to understand just what we have got hold of. I figure this is the most terrific bit of Darwinian news ever. Right?'

'Right.'

'Don't leave me out,' cried Thirn, jumping up.

The assembly hall was packed. Noel was effectively in control.

All junk was cleared out of the way. Everyone was revitalised by the discovery of life on Mars, which until now had been merely one of those crazy science-fiction imaginings.

Sitting on the panel were the two doctors, Nivec and Cood. Thirn was also on display.

Nivec opened the proceedings. 'Thanks to the courage of our friend Thirn here, we can say with confidence that yes, there is native life on this planet, although life rather different from that envisaged by Professor Percival Lowell some centuries ago. My colleagues and I wish to give you the scientific background as we understand it at this stage.'

He then spoke of the Permian-Triassic event, some 250 million years ago, when a great percentage of marine and terrestrial genera perished. It seems most probable that this wholesale destruction was caused by more than one violent impact from space. These bolides, passing through the solar system, were unlikely to have impacted Earth alone.

Nivec warned the audience that he was talking hypothetically. But something resembling the P-Tr event could have occurred on Mars, in what might tentatively be labelled the Martian Permian period.

The severity of the event on Earth may be judged by the fact that 30 million years passed before diversity was re-established. On Mars, diversity was never established.

Climbing out of that great pit of extinction were therapsids and later cynodonts, mammal-like reptiles. Cynodonts form part of the long trail that leads to the origins of mankind.

He said that there was a possible resemblance between some therapsids and the creatures just discovered under the Tharsis shield.

'And I discovered them!' shouted Thirn, jumping up and waving her hands above her head. Some in the audience laughed and clapped.

Nivec could not help smiling. 'So you did, and we sha'n't forget it!'

He then went on to emphasise his main point. 'Therapsids evolved and evolution was and still is continuous. Yes, our ancestors came down from the trees, but long before that, more ancient ancestors climbed out of the pit of P-Tr's vast extinction event into the trees. Don't forget that first of all trees had to appear.

'But on Mars, being of lower mass and on the fringes of the comfort zone of the Sun, evolution, we'd guess, proved more difficult. These creatures just discovered by – we know who, don't we? – are Martian equivalents of therapsids, living evidence of a system-calamity Earth has long outgrown.

'I want you to realise that scientific study of the remote past can enlighten us regarding the present. The fact that today's evidence might be edible should not blind us to the discovery we are now about to announce to the whole world.'

AS WE ALWAYS KNEW THERE IS LIFE ON MARS
HEROIC GIRL DISCOVERS HIDDEN LIFE (Pic. p 6)
FOOD FOR THOUGHT ON RED-HOT PLANET
SCI-FI COMES TRUE

One person was not at the lecture. He had other things to attend to. Tad had moved into the Chinese tower with Gongcha. Gongcha had put her deputy in charge, so that her affair with Tad would not be interrupted.

It was important to both Gongcha and Tad that he should be kissing the enchanting dimples on her behind. He had kissed almost everything else on offer, sometimes thoughtfully, sometimes entirely without thought.

Gongcha had responded ardently, indeed almost acrobatically on occasion.

'I am pleased to be pleasured. If I may play with words?' she asked.

'Oh, you can play in any way – even in ways we haven't tried yet.'

She rolled over on to her back to clutch his prod. 'This poor lonely item! I must give it shelter at once . . .'

Smiling mischievously, she did so, but teasingly slowly.

Tad clutched her tightly. 'Oh, oh, oh, Gongcha, my darling, you prove to me there is life on Mars. Real life . . .'

Nevertheless Chang Mu Gongcha had things on her mind other than sex. An invitation had come from the West tower to inspect the new animals caught in the water course running under the ground between West, China, and on into the unknown.

Gongcha accepted and, at an hour fixed between them, presented herself with Chin Hwa, her chief scientist, and an escort at the gate of West. Noel and a scientist awaited her there. Showing the Chinese Director every courtesy, Noel took her and Chin Hwa to the science laboratories. Here the two captive fish-like things had been transferred to one fair-sized tank. Lights had been lowered to suit the imagined preferences of the pseudo-therapsids.

Nivec appeared, polite and formal. He described briefly the discovery and capture of the creatures, omitting the name of Thirn. He told Chang Mu Gongcha of the theory that these animals, part reptile, part mammal, were the equivalent of the terrestrial therapsids and the later cynodonts existing some 260 million years ago. He made no mention of what might become of the two specimens they had.

There was talk of an expedition to catch more specimens.

Then Nivec bowed and left Gongcha and Chin Hwa to their inspection and her thoughts.

A wooden plank provided by the building department gave the creatures something to rest on. They lay half in and half out of the water, unmoving. As she walked slowly round the tank, their great eyes followed her. Otherwise, they were unmoving, their long bony heads flat against the plank they clutched. Their legs were fin-like, with a firm hold on the plank.

Chin Hwa was making notes into his watputer. 'To categorise these animals as equivalents of ancient Permian animals is premature. No research has been done. We have no evidence of bodily scales on therapsids. These creatures must live in water to obtain their oxygen quota . . .'

Chang Mu Gongcha scarcely listened. She stood looking at the captive fishlike beings. They stared back at her. No trace of emotion from them to her – or, for that matter, from her to them. No repugnance.

She stood with one hand against the tank that contained them, steadying herself against her thoughts.

Their hardship. Their struggle to live. Their need to reproduce. Their instinct to continue. Their deaths, of course. Whatever passed through their heads by way of response to their environment.

What was it she found here so horrible, so enduring, so inarticulate? Was it not that these faculties she imagined in them, however dark, however ancient, however alien – all such faculties which rose unbidden to her inner vision – she herself shared, and with all humanity, trapped as they were in time?

She turned finally to Chin Hwa. 'Record that we saw them alive.'

27
Hitting the Trail

Preparations which kept Gerint busy were well under way for the monthly exploration. He was not one to allow those confounded therapsids to disrupt his routine.

The first exploration team had checked that underground water source first plumbed by the android drill. They had sent down a plumb line. The water was of considerable depth; but they could not gauge the size of the chamber containing the water. The question of whether to send down a diver, thus necessarily boring a larger hole, had been postponed and then somehow forgotten.

Gerint said nothing, not even to his partness, Dr Gior, but inwardly he raged to reflect that he could have gone down into the waters himself. He would then have had the honour of being the discoverer of Martian life, rather than that silly little creature, Thirn. She lacked dignity.

Meanwhile, under his supervision, two dozen people, men and women, masked up and hit the trail. One objective was to maintain contact with the planet itself. There was also the hope of finding something of an answer, or a new question, with which to intrigue the scientific community back on Earth – something which might keep UU investments flowing.

The expedition set out in the Martian afternoon. The first expeditions had been linked together by lightweight cable. It had proved inconvenient. Now they spread out, all keeping within sight of each other – not, as they laughingly said, that they were afraid of encountering little green men, but rather to combat a feeling of utter isolation which confronted them. Shadows of sunset gathered, reinforcing the isolation. They were moving into hitherto unexplored territory.

Humans are social animals. Here on these desolate slopes, even within sight of others, loneliness confronted them.

They moved over the dusty surface in the direction of the volcano Ceraunius Tholis. Every now and then they came across small round pits created by incoming space stones, all of which they examined.

Whereas the orbit of Earth performed almost a regular circle round the Sun, Mars' orbit was more elliptical. The distances between the two planets were variable. When they were on opposite sides of the Sun in superior conjunction, the distance between them amounted to some fifty-five million miles. When Earth passed between Mars and the Sun, in opposition, the distance might be as little as four million miles. In other words, the time in which Earth brightened and faded was governed by planetary orbital motions.

Nothing is simple. Dust storms frequently arose when no expeditions could be undertaken. This expedition took place towards the end of spring, when all was still and the skies clear. The sun shone, a small disc shedding a pennyworth of light, and sinking towards the horizon. Earth could not be seen. The little moon Diemos was high, hardly noticeable against the backdrop of stars. Phobos would soon be rising.

No storms. No wind. No sound. Silence like eternity. Silence scarcely broken by the scrape of a couple of dozen boots tramping over regolith.

All told, the men and women of the expedition moved in a melancholy tranquillity, as they headed slowly northwards. Most agreed the scene was not without beauty, inducing a feeling as yet unnamed, compounded of regret and delight. The intensity of this sensation spread comparative silence between the expedition members. Although an indifference to religion had lured them here, they were overcome by a sense of sanctity.

Later, back in the tower when their heavy togs were removed, this indefinable sensation would be discussed and, if possible, given a name. One suggestion so far, compounded from Greek roots, was metanipoko, created from words for regret and sublimity. *Metanipoko.*

Reaching Ceraunius, they climbed the west wall of the volcano, Gerint leading. They stumbled up a wide crack which served as a kind of pathway. On Earth, the climb would have been arduous. Here, it was pleasant enough. They had climbed back into the lees of sunset.

Nearing the broken lip of the volcano, they found rubble of shattered lava-rock. A short distance on and this changed into parallel seams of rock resembling strings of beads.

'Here's something!' Vooky exclaimed. 'A fish, by the look of it.'

They crowded round, bending as much as the stiff yixiing huaheng suits permitted. Certainly there, in one of several rope-like strings of rock, was a fish shape: featureless, lacking head or fins, but fish-shaped certainly . . . An infant therapsid, perhaps?

A torchlight was shone on it. Vooky cried, 'Yes, we've found it! Past life! Oh, what luck! Almost as crucial as those things . . .!'

Another woman was beginning to scratch at the rock with a knife.

'Don't be too hasty, dear. This shape is also the shape of a leaf. It's no fish –'

'It is a fish,' Vooky insisted. 'How can you be so stupid? What would a solitary leaf be doing on Ceraunius?'

A man joined in, asking what a solitary fish would be doing here on Ceraunius. So an argument developed, polite, cool, but growing warmer.

Vooky suddenly shifted her position. How could a small fish have got to the mouth of a volcano? she asked. In any case, this fish-like, leaf-like shape was common enough, in organic or inorganic nature. Hope had driven her to make an error. She apologised to all concerned.

'After seeing these other things, you know – thrapsids, does he call them? I mean you can't help wondering what else . . . well, you never know. Anyhow, sorry!'

'Never mind,' said Gerint.

They stood in silence, in the enveloping stillness, looking at their boots or down on to the plain.

Overhead, the rich blackness of unending space, the faint light of stars. Distantly, a comet moved, heading farther into the system, towards the Sun.

Eventually they made their way back to the West tower. Hope was such a hateful weakness. It sang out, sprang out, when least expected.

Out of nowhere, heading for the sun. Like the comet.

After the expedition's return, both sexes showered together. Then the usual corporate conversation was held. They wasted some time agonising over the fish-like rock, talking about archetypal shapes. They discussed what they should call the new emotion many of them experienced on this occasion when walking on Mars. Eventually they decided to adopt *metanipoko*. An intensity of regret and delight.

Stroy ventured to suggest *selbsthilfloszwang*. It was considered but not adopted. Stroy thought to herself that people did not care to admit they found themselves forced to do something.

Several people came up to Stroy after the meeting to say they regretted her new word had not been adopted. Some had felt that unpronounceable word applied to themselves . . .

A neuroscientist and scientific adviser called Lock said, 'We know how quantum coherence plays a part in biological systems. Neurons plus connecting synapses do a job similar to that of transistors. A steady environmental change may act like a switch on our consciousness and our extended consciousness – by which I mean digesting new data and promoting intelligent processing. I'll go along with *metanipoko* provided you all realise we are going to need a quiver full of coinages properly to comprehend our new life-mode.'

Clomp.

Carn raised her voice above several others to suggest that neuroanatomy had been in some way disturbed by the distancing from

156

Earth; new phraseology would be needed for new and emergent aspects.

Noel thumped on the table. 'I want us to look outward. We living here have a new order imposed on us to which we must adapt. It's not easy. We are inclined to mistake a blob of rock for a fish or leaf, although we "know" – in quotes – neither of them ever existed on Mars.'

Lock agreed. 'Our new discoveries cannot by rights be called therapsids. Therapsids existed on Earth long ago. They have no possible link with these creatures here.'

Then she added, 'Remember how mankind in past ages tried in a similar way to impose their order on heavenly bodies. We still talk of galaxies. Wasn't the original word "galaxy" meant to designate the milk spurted from the breast of some daft Greek goddess?'

Clomp.

Their conversation had been punctuated by faint thumpings from below.

Sheea said, 'This talk is fine, but Mars has imposed its order on us. You could say we are not meant to be here. Our brains are fine, our bodies less fine, maybe. But we are talking about the harshness of nature, or should be. These so-called therapsids can reproduce, that's obvious, but they belong here. Nature will not allow *us* to have living babies. It is saying: "This is not your place in the universe – you can't stay here."'

Clang!

'We have deep sympathy for your loss, Sheea. We know it hurts. It hurts all of us.' This was one of the maintenance staff speaking. 'But can you hear that noise from below? You know what that is? The guys are welding together a kind of centrifuge. A roundabout, if you want a friendlier term. A roundabout in which pregnant women can ride – we hope in comfort – and by centrifugal force remedy the lack of gravity.

'And so produce normal living children.'

Clomp.

The days, the watches went by.

28
Some Problem for Mangalian

Noel and Daark were talking, sitting face-to-face across a table in Noel's room. 'The mock-therapsids. An extraordinary discovery, don't you agree?'

'The Permian made flesh,' said Daark. 'Opens up new lines of enquiry.'

'We now have to face a fresh problem,' said Noel, 'but I want us to be prepared. Scientists of all shades are going to want us to ship our mock-therapsids to Earth labs for examination and classification –'

'And of course display,' Daark cut in.

'A discovery beyond imagining. And we don't know what else lurks in the subterranean water courses. Let's suppose the scientific elite are going to send a group here to examine these creatures in situ.

'We must take advantage of this discovery – decide now how we are to approach the question. For instance, should we bargain for better food supplies in exchange for the animals? Of course, resources here being limited, it would be best scientifically to have the creatures removed to a well-equipped terrestrial research centre.'

Daark chewed a thumb nail. 'Does the question even arise? I mean, we are dependent on – owned by, really – the UU. Can't the UU simply lay claim to possession of these mock-therapsids?'

'Then we must engage in delaying tactics, in order to improve conditions here.'

Silence fell between them.

Daark's thoughts drifted. Outside his window where he had worked back on Earth, a ranunculus had grown. Its leaves were heart-shaped and of a dark green. He remembered them when the leaves were damp with dew, just before the first gentle touch of autumn changed them.

Armed with what he had recently been told by Iggog, he was also thinking – was it thinking? – of Noel, of Rosemary Cavendish, of her body, her personality, her smiles, her gestures. Of being intimate with her. He found he was so close to her, and here they were, talking of those things of the deep past they had discovered. Was there something Noel had missed, was waiting for, hoping, before the autumn changed her leaves?

One of her arms, her hands, lay on the edge of the table. How intimate that hand was with all parts of her body. Why had either of them come to this sterile place? What had they been escaping? Why? What did they most deeply, intensely, hope for: for they could not just be, like the leaves of the ranunculus; there must be something moving, deeper, something inexpressible, nevertheless being expressed by the silence between them, as they looked at each other.

He reached out his hand and laid it on Noel's arm.

Smiling, blinking with a quick flutter of eyelids, she withdrew the arm. '"Bride of Christ",' she murmured, with a smile.

Then Daark said, 'I have a related matter I need to ask you.' He felt his voice to be dull, dragged out.

'I recently had a disturbing conversation. With a Know-All. She made several claims, some clearly false, but mainly that the selections of who came to Mars were corrupt. We were not the elite but the outcast – for one reason or another. Do you know anything about that?'

'Let me answer that in a moment. Any other imputations?'

Daark looked down at the table top. 'There was some slander, which I did not believe for a moment. For instance – I'm sorry to repeat this, dear Noel – that you had been having an affair with Mangalian . . .'

Noel rested her elbow on the table and her forehead in her spread right hand. After a long pause, she said, 'I would it had been so. Yes, I loved the man. But he was married. I had to conceal my love . . . Well, perhaps not had to, but I did conceal it . . .'

Neither of them spoke for a while.

Noel said, 'Your scandal-monger – I believe I know to whom you refer, by the way – did have something to sniff out. Mangalian and I had this project, which ran alongside the main aims of the UU. We kept it secret because it concerned – well, it concerned instinct and intuition. Those qualities were appropriate for study even within these confines and I still report on them. That's maybe why we seem more involved with each other than we should otherwise be.'

Daark frowned. 'Sorry, intuition . . .?'

'Our instinctual response to others, to strangers or to those we love. Suppose you are walking along a street. Someone is coming towards you. A stranger. In an instant, you decide how to greet them. "Hello", "Hi" or "Good morning". Or just "Morning". Or you say nothing and pass by in silence. Why? How?

'What's at work? Does it hark back to the times when the stranger might have had a cudgel behind his back?'

'Mmm . . . Similarly in conversation, I suppose?'

Noel said, 'I knew a learned German professor in our university studying the amygdala. He would say that in one of those instances such as I have mentioned, the amygdala mind-shifts us back into the past. He posits that the amygdala served as a brain in the centuries before the neocortex developed. It does seem we have a potential for a kind of mental time-travel.'

The ranunculus, Daark thought.

Noel was saying, 'Hence our liking for past history or novels about it.'

Her shrieker went off. 'Noel? Astronomy is reporting something weird.'

Ficht, back at work, was studying that mysterious globe within the Oort cloud. It was after two in the morning. His comrades had finally retired to their bunks. He had just discovered that Eris had what appeared to be a second small moon orbiting it, and had only just been able to stop himself from re-awakening his colleagues to give them the news. Clutching his head, he walked around the small room in circles. A light caught his eye. He cleared his throat.

He stared at the unexpected dazzle from the north. No, not a comet. What then? It was close. Less than a kilometre away. Ficht could not, dared not, understand it.

He went and roused Rasir who immediately became alert. They stared together at the light.

Judging by its direction they knew what it must be. The Sud-Am tower was burning. The flames jutted out sideways from the upper storeys to be immediately chopped, as by a knife. The fire lived on the oxygen in the tower but died in the all but airless conditions outside.

Rasir ran and sounded the alarm while Ficht dithered. Rasir took the high-speed elevator down to ground level.

The alarm had woken others, who were milling about trying to decide what to do. Herb shouted, 'What if we catch fire from it?'

'Oh, be quiet, man. How could it possibly burn another tower? There's no carrier for the flame, is there?' That was Ooma.

Lock agreed. 'Listen, everyone. This is a crisis, for the Martians in Sud-Am of course, but also for us. What do we do about it? Keep quiet unless you have a suggestion to make.'

'How can we possibly help them?' Carn said. 'We don't have sufficient water available. Nor do we have hoses that stretch that far. We are useless as a fire brigade.'

'I have to point out,' said Doran, in his usual casual manner, 'that the fire will consume all the oxygen in the building in less time than a horse might take to get there at a gallop.'

'But that means everyone there will die,' exclaimed Stroy.

'I couldn't have put it better myself,' Doran said.

'Some people may escape in masks,' said Noel. She had come straight to the scene, and still wore her night overalls.

The crowd stood there mute. They had something new and uncomfortable to think about.

San Diego was a city and port on the south-west coast of North America. It had suffered less from the prevailing recession than many another city, since the shipping trade had revived. Those who took to the air in planes were felt to be in constant danger, since forces known as MEida had developed deadly missiles which ignited fuel tanks on planes, even when fired from a great distance: for example from the icy north of West Canada.

Travel by fast car also had its perils, since the mines which plagued much of the world were now being planted across the States. This despite constant police patrols (which, after a recent incident, were now themselves under suspicion).

The States had never before experienced such misery. Nevertheless Mangalian, alive despite the gossip to the contrary, spoke to the assembly gathered in San Diego's city hall in a spirit of optimism and in fluent Spanish.

'This great country will prevail, as it has prevailed against enemies on many other occasions. True, you now have battles to fight on your own territory in the Eastern states, but there I am confident you shall triumph and will be strengthened by the struggle.

'Your duty is not only to support the troops, but to maintain those liberal philosophies for which the civilized world respects you. Let me give you one example. An example that's bang up to date.

'I'm speaking of your, of our, colonisation of Mars. To many people, the funding of this bold development merely weakens our best universities. I hold that our claim on Mars as habitation is a natural advance which has to be made while we can. Nevertheless, a scientific approach does not mean a neglect of moral responsibilities.

'We see already a new facet to Martian history which tells us much about the vulnerability of the solar planetary system. When we have received more detail we shall gain a better understanding of the Ordovician and its fauna.

'But first we have another more urgent question before us.

'One of the foreign towers has broken rules of conduct we established after long discussion, and in consequence has come to grief. A fire broke out which has destroyed the Sud-Am tower, the occupants of which must be held guilty of transgression. However, we cannot set ourselves up as judges. We must give what succour we can. I have consequently sent a message ordering the West tower to take in survivors of this catastrophe, knowing those courageous spirits will do as I say.

'On another matter . . .' Mangalian paused, gratified by the murmurs of assent his declaration was receiving, ignoring those who scowled and did not clap.

When the assembly was over, Mangalian and his bodyguards escaped from the great room by a side door. Mangalian had done what he saw as his duty and did not wish to answer questions or be interrogated by the press.

His bodyguard, 'Rhino' Ray Saskace, was new to the job and showed himself to be effective in his role. They hurried down a badly-lit side passage.

'Turn here!' said Rhino, taking Mangalian's elbow. 'Safer this way! I got an auto waiting.'

Guided by Rhino, Mangalian took an even narrower side passage. It too was dimly lit. At the far end of it, seen in silhouette, stood a uniformed man.

Suddenly, Mangalian felt a chill of warning. He stopped. Could be the amygdala had whispered in his ear.

'I left my notebook behind,' he said.

Even as he turned to run back, Rhino flung a strong arm about his neck, wrenching him off his feet and putting a knee in the small of his back. The uniformed man rushed to help Rhino.

Between them they carried the struggling Mangalian to the nearest exit, to an untidy yard, behind the great bulk of the town hall, where a truck was waiting, its engine running.

'We'll teach you to drain the university dry,' grunted Rhino. 'Your mouth's too big, that's your trouble.'

They slung him into the rear of the waiting truck.

Mangalian was not seen alive again.

29

Questions of Evolution

The sickening news of Mangalian's death, now only too real, had still to reach Tharsis, when a small matter arose which had to be dealt with. Sheea had reported to the sick bay with a black eye. The pupil of the eye had possibly been damaged. Sheea, more than a year after her loss, still suffered depression; at the show of sick bay compassion, she broke down in tears.

Gossip immediately started.

'No doubt this is the work of Phipp,' said Lock, who even on the ship had shown herself to be no friend of the man. 'He should be locked up.'

'It's that same old problem still bugging Phipp,' Herrit said. 'Sheea refuses to say who made her pregnant. Finally, Phipp lost it, and hit her – hard.

'He *does* suffer from jealousy.'

'Typical male,' joked Rasir. 'Can't get our own way, so hit out. We men always cause trouble. The Chinese have got their figures right – ninety percent of them in their tower are female.'

'And the head of them, Gongcha, is in love with one of our males,' said Stroy. 'The trouble with men is too much testosterone – over-active testicles.'

'We understand you almost came in touch with the largest prod on record.'

Stroy laughed. 'Almost but not quite. Now I wish I had had a look at it! His problem must be some kind of lack of male hormone plus elephantiasis.'

'In other ways, Ficht seems a fairly normal man, and he's got a high I.Q. Why does he want to show his prod about? Is it despair or is it pride?'

'Generally, men flash their prods about from pride or lust.'

'And why must we be so private about our privates?' Rasir asked.

'Well, I've often wondered whether men will be disappointed when they see this precious secret thing of ours,' offered Stroy.

Noel's musing were on a different level. 'Women rarely fight among themselves, although it does happen. Men are stronger, presumably an indication that they were born to hunt. Men fight. Men have something they need to achieve. Manhood. Armies have traditionally been for men only. Brave men. It's a way of initiation into male company, presumably a hangover from early days in tribal Africa, where a youth had to go out and kill a lion with his bare hands, or fuck a female gorilla . . .'

'Yeah, with a bare prodkin start it all . . .'

Stroy said, 'I've always understood that male and female psychol-ogies are more similar than different. That's why the diverse psychologies can submerge happily into one – during a love affair, for instance – at least for a while.'

Noel nodded curtly and returned to her quarters. She had a woman sharing the sleeping arrangements, but did not greatly enjoy her loss of privacy.

Rasir remained interested in the conversation concerning diverse psychologies.

'Witness Tad and Gongcha,' he said. There was laughter – some of it rather envious – round the table.

'What do you mean, "witness"? Are you a Peeping Tom?'

'Pity there's no third sex,' Stroy said. 'The more sex the better.'

'What would a third sex do?'

'It could act as umpire . . .'

'Oh, I was as sick as a – what gets frightfully sick? – sick as a pig. I would never go through that again.' Tuot was telling Daark of her experience in the new pregnancy roundabout. She went on to elaborate just how sick she had been and the other pregnant girls too.

'So we're back to square one again,' said Daark, cutting her short.

'It's funny, 'cos Mars is rotating and that doesn't make us sick,' said Tuot.

'We ought to go down to the basement and consult the engineers. Maybe they could adjust the speed.'

Tuot shuddered dramatically. 'I wouldn't go back in there for all the tea in China. As for that little rapscallion, Squirrel . . .'

A day after the fire, and the beginning of Martian summer, there were still some survivors of the Sud-Am catastrophe outside the West tower and other towers, huddling around spare air tanks they'd either recovered, or been given. Somehow they seemed just a cloud on the horizon. Meanwhile, the catastrophe itself cast gloom over the occupants of the West tower. Aymee wanted to discuss the case, knowing a decision was urgent.

'We are all upset about the fire at Sud-Am tower. Many people have perished, people like us. Surely, we must do something regarding this unhappy situation.

'We await instructions from UU. Why is that? Does kindness need instruction?'

She snorted in a minor key. 'But we are too busy fixing the water filter now we've seen the critters that pee in it . . .

'And of course Thirn has been bathing in it . . .'

'Meanwhile, we don't forget the more serious and abiding problem facing us, our inability to reproduce on this benighted planet. Dying now in a fire, or dying at some point in the future – this whole mission's a waste if we don't have children. The whole prospect of exploration of the solar system hinges on our bringing forth a new generation – a generation not native to Earth.

'Shortly before we left Luna for Mars,' Aymee said, 'I went to see an opera by Lyizaz called *Steel to Saturn*. The music was remarkable but the story, as so often is the case in opera, is absurd. Our hero falls in love with a mysterious woman who has arrived on Earth from the moons of Saturn. As it happens, our hero's son, Cando, has gone into space and nothing has ever been heard of him since.

'When there is a terrible storm – with much use of cymbals – our hero rescues the mysterious woman from a flood. They make love and only afterwards does she reveal that she is a metal being.

'They have an all-metal child and then go to the mother's home on Titan, the moon of Saturn where her kind live. Our hero finds that his son is living safely there. Everyone rejoices. The end!'

Many people in the auditorium laughed with scorn.

Aymee continued. 'You don't need me to tell you that, although the singing is good, the music beautiful and the scenery ingenious, the story is as soppy as can be. Leo Tolstoy in his essay "What is Art?" mocks an opera with a similar kind of plot. Disguises are generally needed to drag us through three acts.

'But think again of *Steel to Saturn*. Perhaps there is some meaning to it after all. We may need to change – I mean change our natures – to get to the further planets. To mutate. Indeed, we may be undergoing a terrible storm, the death of all our precious babies, before we are fit to travel further, as we hope to do, if only as far as Jupiter and its moons.

'Evolution is a continuous process. We see many examples. Can anyone offer me an example?'

Doran was the first to respond. 'It happens I was born in a non-country, a kind of evolution in its own right. My country had been called Yugoslavia. Everywhere was still unsettled and my family took me to live on a Croatian island. The lizards there had developed a stronger jaw-movement – bite, in other words – than the lizards on neighbouring islands, because the vegetation was lusher and stronger. Indeed, one of them bit me. I can vouch for the stronger bite . . .'

He spoke in his usual rather off-hand way. While the audience was chuckling at his last remark, Doran added, 'I suppose better known than my agony, for which evolution is to blame, there's the case of the African elephant and its shorter tusks, that Daark spoke of before.'

Others started shouting that bacteria were surviving antibiotics at an alarming rate.

Aymee held up her hands. 'Okay, that will do. We can't find any cure for the stillborn baby syndrome, but it *will* be solved for us. Just wait for five years. Our wombs will have adapted to the environment. Think of the womb as an elephant's tusk! Our foetuses will also have figured things out. We shall be child-rich. I'm taking bets!'

To her amazement, the audience began cheering.

It seemed they would never stop.

It came as a surprise to Aymee to find that even the most learned of her companions had not read Darwin's *Origin of Species*, although they understood and took Darwin's conclusions for granted. She had a grand old book by Alan Moorehead on disc. She played this disc to those who would listen. Many of them were particularly interested in what was said about Darwin's discoveries when the *Beagle* was moored in the Galapagos Islands.

"The finches were dull to look at, and made dreary unmusical calls. All had short tails, built nests with roofs, and laid white eggs spotted with pink, four to a clutch. Their plumage varied within limits: it ranged from lava black to green, according to their habitat . . .

"It was the variety of their beaks that so amazed Darwin. Clearly the birds had found different foods available on different islands. By this time he must have realised that he was on the edge of a remarkable and disturbing discovery . . ."

'You see,' Aymee said, 'we are like the finches – "according to their habitat" – on the edge of an evolutionary brink. These therapsid-creatures are old. We are new! Be proud!'

Among those not attending this discussion were three persons in particular, Noel, who still awaited word from UU on what they should do for the Sud-Am refugees; Ficht, whose break time it was, and who slept in his bunk with his penis lying along his leg like a tame snake; and Tad, who was cuddled up with his ivory-skinned love, Chang Mu Gongcha, lying face to face, taking in her breath and her beauty.

It would hardly have interested this pair of lovers, who had grown so close, to read in Darwin's *The Descent of Man* that 'the mental characteristics (of races) are likewise very distinct; chiefly as it would appear in their emotional, but partly in their intellectual faculties.'

As for their physical and sexual differences, it was largely this exoticism which attracted the one to the other: xenophobia stood on its head.

Lock was a quiet woman, but here she was moved to comment on Aymee's final point. 'After humanity emerged from Africa, some tribes went to Europe and some to Asia. Those who journeyed to the West found a forested terrain. Those who journeyed eastwards found the bamboo, that invaluable and versatile plant.

'These two groups were apart from each other – hardly known to each other – for many centuries. They did finally meet, Netherlanders and British on one hand, Chinese on the other. Had they failed to meet for only a few millennia more, geography would have seen to it that two subspecies developed.

'Meaning what? Meaning that cohabitation and copulation would have remained possible but the production of children – just as in our case here and now – might have been non-viable.

'So every time love-making between East and West takes place, it marks a unity between the two contrasting environments, and a celebration of it.'

From the audience came a woman's voice, asking what of those who went neither east nor west but north.

Lock suddenly recalled a lewd joke from her school days in Estonia. Putting on a Continental accent, she said, 'Lucky Alphonse, he is in ze middle . . .'

30
Precious Discoveries

Another expedition was preparing to set out, leaving by the rear exit of the tower to avoid survivors of the Sud-Am catastrophe – there was an unspoken guilt that they had done nothing to help them for days. Noel, having finally learned of Mangalian's death, received a message from him on her private squealer. An underling or substitute must have forwarded it belatedly. Noel hesitated before opening it. Her heart beat faster since, despite the chiding tone of the message, she believed she heard in it a response to her love for him, the one man for whom she had felt any deep sexual warmth.

The message said: 'You know as well as anyone the need for change, for improvement, in the human species – improvement in particular in moral qualities. Of course we understand the dangers from disease of contact with the pet-loving Sud-Ams. Nevertheless, such is our hope, our thirst – which I know you share, dear Noel – for our moral growth, the West must, absolutely must, give those sad survivors refuge at once, however the West tower may suffer as a result.

'My hope and heart are with you. Mangalian.'

His voice ceased.

Noel flung the pod against the wall. As it fell to the floor, she rushed over and trampled on it.

'The hypocrite!' she cried. 'Why should we who are healthy embrace those who are sick? Are we who are here not in danger enough? I'll have none of it. He can keep his damned heroism in his grave!'

Later she announced to all and sundry that orders had come from UU not to let a single Sud-Am refugee into the tower.

'They brought disaster on themselves by deliberately disobeying the rules regarding the keeping of pets. So they must suffer from the infringement. Our lives are harsh enough.'

This announcement was in general greeted with relief, but there were more than a few who saw the edict as defying all that true civilization stood for.

Worse was to follow. A terse report arrived, on two suicide bombs exploding in quick succession inside Harvard University buildings. The oldest American university, founded by an English settler in the Seventeenth Century, was forced to close its doors to allow extensive restoration to take place. All external funding was temporarily placed on hold, including the bi-annual contribution to the UU.

Then another report, following the first report only a few minutes later. It announced briefly that the results of Herbert Ibn Saud Mangalian's post-mortem revealed that he had been tortured before death.

Reading this latest report, Noel found herself torn apart. She picked up the pod she had trampled and kissed it before stowing it away in a drawer.

Many other inhabitants of the tower had cried at Mangalian's death, some hiding their tears, some proud to show them.

The Mars colony and the UU itself were now in deep trouble, despite the excitement caused by the discovery of Martian life.

Haddod in the observatory, clutching his folded arms to his chest, said, 'We're sunk, aren't we? They're bound to let us down now.'

'What is more disgraceful,' Ficht replied, 'is that behind the project which brought us to Mars was the hope, even an expectation, of getting to the moons of Jupiter. Two more generations of technological development and I believe we would have made it.'

'Huh. So what now?' Haddod hardly expected an answer, but Ficht provided one. 'As far as I can see, the alternatives are simply that we – or most of us – get ferried back to Earth. Rescued. Or that we are all left here to rot. Shipwrecked. The latter alternative is decidedly the more likely of the two.'

All up and down the tower, people were coming to the same conclusion. Robinson Crusoe had had it easy.

Now every man and woman in the crowd experienced themselves as solitary beings, each with a finite life span, faced with failure. Muttering perhaps a phrase to themselves over and over:

Future like a blank beach
Always this same sad half-light
Why didn't I screw her when I had the chance?
My 'Petty Proceedings' – who will remember it?
Why did I say 'No' to him that lecherous night?
Something in me I cannot reach
Oh, mother dear, you'll need a carer soon
I kissed her. I felt her. Oh, her juice, her breath . . .
My boundaries dissolving into the blankness
At least we're all – all heroes. Trail-blazers
Metanipoko, yes, regret, sublimity, at least we've known it
'Mars as the Abode of Death' . . .
Sea lavender, the beach, little white shells, the tide coming
     in fast
What is it to die? Far lesser thing than living
Too bad living doesn't last.

But Gerint was a single-minded man, who kept on doggedly. His preparations for the next expedition were almost complete. Only the oxygen cylinders remained to be charged, and that would be done immediately before they set out. Sensing that there might never be the opportunity for another expedition, Gerint himself was determined to go on this one.

'Come on, girls! This is going to be the expedition to end all expeditions!' He escorted his partness, pretty Dr Gior into his office and locked the door. She was already taking down her overalls.

'Darling!' he said. They rushed at each other.

'A quickie,' she said. He went down on her first.

Equipped with masks and wearing tough yixiing huaheng outfits, the company set out, seven women and four men. Leaving by the rear of the tower, they came across a man propped against the wall in a sitting posture.

'He's sick,' said Rooy.

'He's dead,' said Dr Gior. She could feel no compassion as the hormones of sex still streamed in her mind.

As he prodded the body, Rooy saw that fire had burnt much of the man's clothes. It was clear that this was a Sud-Am body. In the almost complete vacuum, corruption would be slow to gain a hold.

With Mons Olympus distant at their backs, the group made their way south-eastward, across a strip of Hesperian-age flow plain. The going was slow. They had not explored in this direction before. Several of them thought there was nothing new to be discovered.

Many flows could be traced for a mile or more. Some of them, coalescing, formed broad overlapping sheets, where progress was easier. Not that ease was exactly what they sought.

The flows sometimes gave way to low-cratered territory, where some ruined crater walls were reminiscent of ruined terrestrial castles. Some of the going here was dangerous, where half-concealed channels ran, shadows adding to the difficulties of negotiation. Gerint himself, his mind part preoccupied with other things, slipped and fell into one such channel. A cloud of dust stirred up about him.

The other members of the group, once they saw that Gerint was unharmed, moved back, avoiding the dust. Gerint heaved himself on to his hands and knees. He felt what he took for pebbles. Taking hold of one, he brought up into the uncertain light a green stone.

He was about to throw it away when Stroy told him to hang on and jumped down into the channel with him.

'It could be valuable,' she said.

'But not on Mars!'

'No, it's a – hell, I forget the name.'

Stroy began digging with her hands. Soon she brought up another green stone, similar to the first one but slightly larger.

Another plunge and up came a blue-ish stone, and then another. These stones she held up to the light. They glittered with a purple richness.

'You know what these are?' she asked. 'Tanzanite! That's the name! Unless I'm mistaken, this purple stone is known as Tanzanite. I came across it in Jaipur when I was working there. It's quite precious. We'll take this lot back and look them up. They should fetch a good price.'

As he climbed out of his hole, Gerint said, 'They're worth nothing here.'

'Have you never heard of the export business?'

The group went no further. They turned back for the tower.

The Sud-Am corpse was still sitting by the rear door where they had left him, quite elegant in death.

Stroy laid the jewels on the desk before her while the others watched. Gior picked one up, polished it, held it close to her eye.

A wakipurr produced figures concerning the stones.

Tsavorite, also known as green grossularite, of the garnet family – a stone has recently fetched up to $9000 per carat, on account of its rarity – 1000 times rarer than diamond.

Tanzanite (pronounced tan-zan-ite), a variety of the gemstone zoisite, can appear blue or purple or yellow from different angles. Stones of Tanzanite have been fetching up to $4000 per carat, on Earth, in spite of depression and deflation.

Some geologists believe these rare stones were formed more than 580 million years ago.

'Five hundred and eighty million years ago!' Stroy breathed. 'How I adore such incomprehensible bundles of time . . .'

'This could be the saving of us,' said Noel, withholding the excitement from her voice. 'We need as many of these jewels as we can gather. Gerint, can you form up another expedition at once to collect as many of these precious objects as possible? You all realise, don't you, that with these – well, these amazing gifts – we could buy our own university?'

All present beamed at one another. Later, it was Noel alone who, thinking of Mangalian, wept to herself. She determined that if the precious stones fetched the prices they hoped for, she would use some of the money to pay for the erection of a statue at the tower gate to commemorate Mangalian and his work.

In the end, only one consignment of precious stones made it back to Earth. As the transport ship returned from that first round trip with enough supplies for several decades, and bearing a delegation of biologists, and as Herb stowed away in the opposite direction, lines of communication suddenly dropped. The worst fears of the Tower dwellers were realised, in their moment of triumph.

Earth's fate remained a mystery. Eventually, after months of panic and recrimination, the thoughts of all in the towers turned to survival.

Long slow Martian years had passed. Once again, as of yore, Aymee and Rooy were enjoying their daily walk and exercise.

The lighter gravity of this world, which had proved such a barrier when colonisation began, was now proving a blessing. That taxation of weight which bears earthlings to early graves was in part alleviated. By terrestrial reckoning, Aymee and Rooy were several centuries old. Here, they bore their age lightly. Meeting them on their stroll, one might mistake them for reasonably youthful. Aging had not affected fertility, conception was as easy as ever. Foetuses were getting stronger and staying longer in the womb. The stillbirth problem was not yet resolved, but all had a sense that soon, soon this would change. *They* had adapted to Mars, children must be next. They had time.

Change marked their surroundings. Over the long chilly years, oxygen manufacture had been increased. The towers had developed and expanded, but no more had been built.

Now, beside the path where the couple were walking, vegetation grew. That vegetation was of a kind which, long ago, had fuelled and fed the ancient dynasties of China, the bamboo.

The venerable couple passed Gongcha and Tad, riding in a carefree way on a light tractor.

As it happened, Rooy and Aymee were going in one direction and the younger pair in the other.

And so it transpired, appropriately enough, that it was this younger pair who were about to encounter – as a later phrase had it – 'History riding in the guise of the Future'.

31
Visitors

The light was light enough, the stars – for there was no sky within the meaning of the word – gleamed in rich darkness overhead.

Gongcha and Tad were riding in a light tractor borrowed from the Works Dept of the Chinese tower. They were heading for Olympus Mons, always one of the dominant features of Mars as seen from Earth, a volcano with a vast aureole.

'It reminds me of my own breast,' said Gongcha, smiling. 'Which reminds me of a most peculiar dream I had in the night. Imagine a very crowded street, with people jammed on the sidewalks on either side. An open carriage of an unfashionable kind is coming slowly along the road. In the carriage is the most beautiful princess. Are you listening, Tad?'

'Oh, sorry, yes. Go on.'

'You were there. And in my dream, I was telling you my dream, dictating it as it happened, and you kept saying that I had told you about it before. But still the carriage kept coming and I was telling you, and the crowd were all saying, quite gently, "Aaaaah!" as if in a single breath. I was puzzled because now the carriage seemed to be going in the opposite direction. But the crowd were not noticing . . . And I kept telling you . . . You kept saying I had already told you.'

Gongcha let the tale die away. 'Silly, really. But I was sure it was important.'

'Uh huh, okay.'

'You might at least pretend to listen,' she said, without malice.

Tad stopped the tractor engine. 'I thought I heard something . . . A – I don't know what. You think this dream of yours all happened on Mars?' He found he was trembling.

'Oh, I am convinced of it. But not this Mars.'

'There it is again. Listen!'

Sound did not carry, yet this sound carried. Two notes together. And then . . . they couldn't understand it . . .

And then a vehicle was low overhead, shaped like a surf board, but studded along the base, much like the tentacle of an octopus. It was set on a course that took it round behind Olympus, slowing all the while. The pair were like children again, clasping each other's hands.

'It's going to land! What shall we do, Tad?' There was curiosity in her tone, salted by alarm.

Tad told her to climb out of the tractor. They both climbed out and stood by the vehicle. Gongcha clung to Tad's arm.

'There's not much we *can* do,' he said. Yet all the time his gaze was sweeping over the tractor, looking for anything that might serve as a weapon. He saw nothing of any use. 'If they're hostile – well, we'd never get back to the tower in time. Just stay put and try not to look alarmed.'

Gongcha's tinkling laugh was nervous. 'But this is *not* an Earth vessel?'

'Where else could it be from?' Even as Tad spoke, he was thinking, *My god, it could be from anywhere.*

The vehicle hovered only a few metres from the pair and then sank to the ground, churning up a cloud of dust and grit. It exuded light all round. 'Don't move,' said Tad, grasping Gongcha's wrist.

'Where exactly do you imagine I might move to?' she asked. ''What's going to happen?'

Something resembling a large tongue stuck out from the floor of the vehicle. Three personages emerged from the flier and walked unhurriedly down. At first they could be seen only in silhouette. When they were farther from their craft more details were discernible. The three of them turned in unison. They wore what appeared to be short tight jackets and baggy knee-length trousers. Their midriffs were bare. Each of them had a silvery leaf-like instrument clipped to one ear. Their complexions were spectrally pale; in contrast, their hair was brown, cut short. All three had high cheekbones and strange features.

Rather more noticeable than any of this, two of the trio carried weapons resembling lances, which were pointed at Tad and Gongcha.

The unarmed member of the trio held up a hand, possibly in greeting, and said something incomprehensible.

'Sorry,' said Tad. He felt that his bones were turning to water. 'We – we understand what – oh, I mean we do not understand what you are saying.' Even as he said it, he shuddered with a thrill of – was it fear or even excitement? – somehow realising he was addressing – well, someone from another world . . . The awe of it made him gasp.

Gongcha spoke up in his stead. 'We are surprised by your arrival. We have our own language and you will hardly expect us to understand yours. This makes communication difficult, if not impossible. So' – she bit her lip uncertainly – 'would you prefer to go away, please?' Gongcha lifted her arms to indicate the possible ease of take-off.

The three arrivals seemed to laugh without showing any amusement on their faces.

Tad registered the shape of their heads, where foreheads protruded above enlarged eyes. He was occupied with their strange beauty when the newcomers began communicating wordlessly.

The communication came in a wave, by way of stars, planets and planetesimals, winds, oceans, currents, swarming cities, cloud features and flights of birds ever a-wing, lifetimes of grandeur and squalor, circumstances and inheritance, and much else Tad could not understand, although he recognised that his misunderstanding was inevitable. Such knowledge came as a whirlwind.

Oh that communication!

This bolt from the blue, from those protruding foreheads, made it clear enough that these visitors were inheritors. Humanity's pained struggle to give birth in alien places had succeeded in only two more fleeting years from that point. Amniotic adjustment, in restoring generation – but many generations later – had resulted in these strangers now visiting; these, standing here now, on the wide pavements of Tharsis.

And she whom Tad loved, coming from another country – he saw she too had received this glorious puzzlement of communication. She and Tad clutched one another in a kind of rapture. 'They're sus–speaking Mandarin!', she gasped.

But rapture and shock. For all the grandeurs of their armies, their artists, their autocrats and kings, humanity – the communication made that at least clear – humanity was but one life form among a myriad more.

Tad recovered himself sufficiently to address them again.

'We are astonished. If you are what you seem, then this is an archi–architival situation. No. I meant to say archetypal. Did I? You look remarkably like us. Many generations ago, our forefathers descended from apes. It may be the same with you . . . Sorry – I'm babbling . . .

'Perhaps you have been mistaken in believing that we speak Language A, when all the time we speak Language B. Since we are residents of this planet, we believe that you should use Language B when in conversation with us. My hope is that you understand my speech after that great wordless – that wordless communication of yours.'

Gongcha stared at him in astonishment. 'What are you on about?'

Tad closed his eyes, still unable fully to believe this meeting was happening.

'This is as incomprehensible as my dream.' Gongcha looked about her but there was no one else to be seen. 'How can we cope after that . . . what was it? The vision they communicated?'

After holding a brief word with one another, two of the three newcomers retreated into their machine. They returned after some minutes – minutes evidently devoted to extrapolation – with what looked like a slender glass booklet. The gadget spoke perfect Mandarin and English.

'Your speech is welcome. We see you are carrying no injurious weapons. That is well. Accompany us to your living place.'

'The rudiments of a living place, at least,' said Tad, as they set off back to the towers, followed by the newcomers, who said nothing more. Their craft followed them. Silent. Alien. Hull just above ground.

Tad clutched Gongcha's arm. 'Can you believe this? Is all this real?'

She was staring at the newcomers. 'Is it destiny? I want to touch one of them. Could this be the irresistible reason – hidden from all of us – why we came to Mars in the first place?'

'I don't understand.'

Then, suddenly agitated, 'Just suppose they turn on us, kill us – know till your dying breath I loved you.'

'Oh and I you, dearest. But these are linguists. Linguists don't kill. Do they?'

'How can I know?' she said. 'But at least that great communication teaches us there are many things we do not understand, even about life itself . . .'

They had to leave their tractor where it stood.

32
Descendants from the Present

They were awaited. Many people had left the five remaining towers spurred by curiosity or apprehension or a combination of both. Above them, above the towers, above Tharsis, now hovered a great grey machine, its nearside flank reflecting the rays of the sun. It was the shape of a slice of melon, although its size was far more grand. It was the main ship, to the shuttle that Tad and Gongsha had encountered.

If the ship was not from Earth, which seemed apparent from the ship's design, then from whence did it come? Was it hostile? Several humanoids emerged from this machine, descending in a mighty elevator, to look about with intense interest.

People continued to emerge cautiously from West and China towers, and then from the more distant towers. They were fearful and stood in small clusters, muttering among themselves. Everyone, it seemed, had received the great enveloping communication.

Silence. No movement. At length, a separate door in the elevator

187

slid open. A small man in saffron robes emerged. On his head he wore a kind of crown from which simulated flames arose. He bore a placard on which were glowing the words:

HAVE NO FEARS – WE ARE THE DESCENDANTS OF YOU PRESENT PEOPLE HERE

Much muttering from the crowd. 'Supposing they are descendants,' Doran said. 'Do they happen to love their parents?' It was a nervous joke, and his lip trembled.

'But if it's true . . .' Tuot's voice was shrill. 'If it's true then the question of childbirth is solved.'

This seminal fact was discussed only later, for now they concentrated on the grand visitors who had appeared from the visiting ship.

An object resembling a sunshade was switched on and one of the visitors held it above the head of the tallest of their group.

This imposing person began addressing the crowd in his native tongue, to the mystification of all. It was Ooma who cried out suddenly, 'Did you hear? He used the word "metanipoko"! Our word! Our coinage!'

The grand person broke off his speech to repeat, smiling, the word 'metanipoko'.

He ran forward and embraced Ooma, then held her shoulders at arm's length.

It was at this juncture that Tad and Gongcha arrived with their escort.

Noel crossed to Tad and was informed that they had managed to speak to the newcomers; but how, she puzzled, had they been able to use this word 'metanipoko', coined here on Tharsis?

'Come on, Noel,' someone interjected from behind her. 'Does it matter? Don't think we're not amazed and absolutely delighted!'

Aided by the translation box, the leading newcomer addressed the crowds still gathering. For some it appeared he spoke in English, but to Gongcha and others who had come out from the China tower to stand silent in wonder his speech was Mandarin.

'We gain pleasure from finding you. I will tell you things of great importance . . .

188

'Perhaps you people here do not realise that the concept of "the universe" is a relic of pre-Copernican thinking. At that time, Earth was supposedly the centre about which the so-called heavenly bodies revolved. Even when the advance of knowledge proved it seriously incorrect, I believe you ancient people continued to use the term for convenience.

'Reality is far larger and more nebulous than you could ever have supposed. Even Einstein long ago declared in his special theory of relativity that time dilation was a possibility. Fast-moving ships will experience time at a different rate to a stationary observer. On our ships, we slow time down almost to a halt.

'It was Noh Ma in your times who laid the foundations for a new understanding of our Reality.

'Gallowan, two centuries ago – our centuries, I fear, not yours – estimated that there were methods whereby a fast-moving body could enter and ride the time spike forward or, indeed, backward. This is what we refer to as the Gallowan Equation or a GE, an adaptation of Noh Ma's work. It would take a day to explain these equations, and then I doubt if you people are entirely equipped to understand. You would require training beforehand.'

'Condescending bastick!' exclaimed Daze. The process that delayed Martian aging to near immortality had slowed the rate of growth from child to adult, too. But, Daze had long been adult now, and was a full and working member of the Martian community.

'But he's probably right,' said Piggy.

Daze raised her hand to ask a question, saying, 'Who is this Noh Ma of whom you speak? Or are we too primitive to hear it?'

The noble person smiled, saying with grave courtesy, 'You may indeed be too primitive for many things, but for sure you have heard the name of the Japanese astrophysicist who first opened the way to Reality space. His name was at one time anglicised. It was Noh Ma Nikasaki.'

The noble person smiled and continued his discourse.

'The modification and application of Gallowan's equation led to the construction of a small working model which they sent backwards in time. It sent us a signal to say we were correct in our calculations. The faster than light trail existed, binding reality together. That was before the model disappeared entirely.'

Gongcha was listening and watching Tad. Tad was listening with his mouth slightly open. Seeing that Gongcha was looking at him, he said in a whisper, 'What power! D'you reckon they'd take us to their future?'

She shrugged, thinking, *Is it power or adventure that arouses him? I can see it's going to be over between us, sooner or later. Alas. In any case . . . Well, I was tiring of him.*

She tuned in to what the noble person was saying.

'. . . building the sizeable vessel which you see anchored above us. When moving, it easily exceeds the so-called speed of light. Passageways winding between the gravitational pull of various solid bodies – they help. So we can travel where we will among star systems. It also means we can travel to the past. As you have just observed . . .'

Gior found herself trembling. At this extraordinary evolutionist moment, she felt they should be hearing the most valiant silver music – and there it was . . .

'Shouldn't we be offering them something?' Gior whispered to Gerint. 'If they're that puissant?'

'What do we have that would not make us appear abject in their eyes?' said Gerint.

The noble person repeated himself, just in case he had not been understood. 'Under Gallowan's and his team's modifications, we are now able to travel to our distant past. With no harm to ourselves.

'You, my friends, primitive though you may be, are our honoured predecessors. Do you understand this? You are our predecessors in the great chain of being. We have developed mentally and bodily. Of the mental aspect I will say that when we converse together, we conjure pictures or pictograms as in groups of words in Chinese scripts.

'These we can alternate as Obscure or Factional, as the situation requires. Our progeny master all such language versions –' here he paused '– I suppose around fifty or fifty-five versions.

'As for bodily development. It is necessary that I show you an example by way of demonstration.'

190

As he spoke, this noble person opened his curiously formed drawers.

A gasp went up from the crowd as his naked flesh was revealed. Wrinkled proboscis-like skin was bisected by a vertical crack where it seemed there was a closed lip of flesh capable of opening when needed.

Reactions were mixed, gasps, laughs, a 'Disgusting!' from Phipp.

Enclosing his remarkable anatomy within his drawers again, the noble person said, 'You may deduce from this development that many years have passed between your lifetimes and ours. And also changing environments.' He spoke plainly, almost with indifference. 'Evolution is a continuous process, improving our survival rates.'

A babble of discussion arose. 'And modesty is extinct,' someone giggled.

'Be quiet!' Herrit shouted. 'We are not Palaeolithics. Hear him out. You men, you find this funny?'

'Why, it's nigh on miraculous . . .'

'Why does he bother?'

'I wish I understood the language shifts he spoke about.'

'I don't like this at all.'

'Oh dear, what's to become of us!'

'Why, this, you ass . . .'

And sundry other comments.

33

Reception in the China Tower

The noble person waited until the shouting died before proceeding to speak again.

'We have become discerning. The ceaseless multiplication of our race is not necessary. Demand must not exceed supply. Do I say that correctly? Too many is too much.

'Humans are no longer divided into two separate sexes, as with you and with those before you in these earlier ages. Or rather, in our generations we carry both sexes within us. For half a year, the masculine comes into play, in the other half the feminine is activated. The conflicts that existed between the sexes, a cause of much friction once, have been annulled; we now experience emotions and sensations from both sides and sensibilities. In my female phase, I can bear children, and have done so. Such is the current reality.'

He listened unmoved to expressions of surprise from the crowd. He stood tall and unmoving. When the crowd grew silent, he continued.

'I believe that even in your day – your Now, which carries you along – it is a commonplace that there exists something of the female in the male and something of the male in the female, in a healthy individual. It's hardly surprising. So that feature has gradually developed from psyche into flesh. This happened long before my grand famoth's time. I trust I make myself clear? All things change, as does the wind.'

After a pause, he said, 'We have been initially surprised to find this planet all but uninhabited. It is easy to shift into conflicting reality veins.'

He had finished, but added smilingly, 'Like you, we live our short and humble lives of four hundred summers and then it's over and done with. Like you, we know well metanipoko . . .'

The noble person and two of his company were shown into the China tower, it being the most decorative of the five towers. The noble person announced himself as Angul Sotor Aret Bila Bilan. He refused the food they offered. He said they took food only at what he called 'the noon of the slight week'. His companions had set a translation box on the table between them.

'It is instructive for us to see Mars Planet in one of its earlier states. You are to be congratulated on preserving it almost unspoiled.'

Noel thanked him for his sentiments.

Gerint asked Angul Sotor Aret Bila Bilan how many planets he had visited.

'I have never been physically on a planet before this time,' came the answer. 'I was born on board our ship. Although I find this floor rather uneven, it is a valued experience to be here.'

Gongcha expressed her surprise. 'Were you happy to be confined on your ship all your life?'

'I was very happy. We have made "happy" one of the constants for usage. It means moderate. I saw many suns and planets and many other manifestations of the cosmos and I had an opportunity to acquire knowledge. In particular some knowledge of Reality.' He seemed to correct himself by adding, 'The shifting sands of Reality . . .'

'So you were never sad?'

He gave a light laugh. 'I was made melancholy when we found a planet where the people were eating native animals and fish, precious denizens of their environment. The lives of such people were spent hunting or killing and slaughtering; the effects pervaded all levels of their societies. We never stayed there. We feared the inhabitants might try to eat us. There was a cult of the knife.'

Tad whispered to Gongcha that he was sick of what he called 'all this rigmarole'. He wished to disappear to consider the grand communication he had received. But she felt differently and felt the need to respond in full to what the great man had said.

'I believe we are carnivores when we get the chance. At least in our generation. Herbivores spend much of their time grazing or browsing, and so do not develop intellect. Also herbivores tend to specialise in their diet, and thus do not spread to other territories, as they might wish. They are more vulnerable to famines or floods.

'In China, we used to have pandas, members of the *Ursidae* family. Their diet consisted almost entirely of bamboo, although some in captivity would eat fish and eggs. But they became extinct because their diets were so limited.'

'They were killed off and eaten,' said Dr Gior sharply.

'Certainly in the terrible time of famine the panda was an easy target, but after that we did our best to preserve the creatures. But their limited habitat could never be ours. We and not pandas have become Martians and Mars-dwellers.'

'Mankind is best considered as an omnivore,' said Gior. 'Hence, in part, our success in spreading. But it does seem that if you stick to vegetables and fruits you are less likely to suffer from various ills – cancer, heart disease, high blood pressure. You may remember that the British used to speak favourably of "the roast beef of old England". That beef was generally washed down with beer. Result – early deaths.'

'Though I have to say,' remarked Dorian in his relaxed manner, 'that I was dining in a vegetarian university in the States once, and they went to the effort of serving me roast beef, but with a glass of water – I could hardly eat the stuff. Give me wine with my meat, every time. Or even without it. Only humans can cook – or serve wine with the joint.'

Angul Sotor Aret Bila Bilan looked confused by this conversation.

'But surely the intestinal length of carnivores –' began Tad, when Noel interrupted. She was not entirely pleased to have to greet manifestly superior visitors. Addressing Angul Sotor Aret Bila Bilan directly, she said, 'Of course we are delighted to have your company here, sir, but tell us the object of your visit?'

'That's easy to guess,' said Squirrel, scoffing. 'To his Lordship we must seem like Stone Age people. This is an archaeological trip they've laid on.'

Angul Sotor Aret Bila Bilan appeared undisturbed by this sarcasm.

'I have heard it said that when strangers arrive somewhere they are suspected of being in some way hostile, or a threat. That is not so in our case. We have every reason to be friendly and helpful to you.'

He waved his hand at one of his comrades, who then spoke.

'We see you have created just enough oxygen for your own needs, and are impressed you've achieved even this with your, I apologise, primitive technology. We present you with an OEM or oxygen-excavation machine. You may inspect it outside. It will bore automatically into volcanic rock and release oxygen to breathe. This will create an oxygen rich environment, which will encourage the birth of healthy children, but also support the population boom you will experience in about three years time. In addition, we would like to present you with cuttings and seeds of various vegetable life which will flourish on Mars, and, incidentally, support your continuing adaptation to this planet.'

Together with his comrades, male or female, Angul Sotor Aret Bila Bilan, gravely bowed to acknowledge reception of the rapturous applause which broke out.

A mere onlooker, Aymee stood with Rooy. She recalled that long ago prophecy of that odd fellow, Herb. What *had* happened to Herb? He had said that strange people would come. Now they had come. Had he then truly been given the gift of prophecy? That Lord of his – which those on Mars did not acknowledge – could there be such a person? Every living thing that ever was had been living, unbeknown to it, in a binary system. Life had existed for millennia. Only in the last two

196

centuries had they known their sun was not alone. Till they saw it, they refused to believe in it. Was this the only thing about which they assumed too much?

Suppose that Lord Herb so revered existed, but could not be seen by mortal eyes . . .

Perhaps she might find a chance to ask Angul Sotor Aret Bila Bilan.

34

A Great Resource

The OEM was installed and began its work immediately. The cuttings and seeds were shared out between the towers. The visitors solemnly said farewell. They allowed themselves to be surrounded by crowds and to be questioned. They smiled with sorrow in their eyes. Yes, there could be questions and in some cases answers; but no more revelations.

The Martian exiles watched as the visitors were carried up in their surf board-like vehicle, up to the mother ship waiting overhead above the towers.

One minute the ship was there, the next it was gone, riding on the Reality track.

'I'm glad no one mentioned the Tanzanite', said Vooky. 'It's surely even more of a resource in their distant time.'

'No, we are the great resource,' said Noel. She looked immensely serious.

It was only when tucked up in her bed that night she fully realised the significance of her own statement. Angul Sotor Aret Bila Bilan and his team had travelled all those millions of light years and centuries to help the little colony on Tharsis because – and she recognised it as one of the bewildering truths of continuing existence – if they, the exiles, her comrades, failed, if the Martian colony failed – there would be no Angul Sotor Aret Bila Bilan, no hope, no human future.

Moved by her own perception, she climbed from her solitary bunk. She stared through the narrow slit of window. There lay the prospect, silent as if waiting.

'We are the great resource,' she repeated to herself.

Appendix

The Unsteady State or, Starting Again from Scratch
By Herbert Ibn Saud Mangalian
A synopsis

The human species has developed so far and no further.

Not so long ago the world was conceived as having two power blocks, East and West. Before the West found itself too rich to fight amongst its interlocking nation states, it carried out wars that were territorial, religious or dynastic, or all three at once. At any one time there were aspects to be praised, others to be condemned.

Some in the West conceived of China, proud representative of the East, as peaceful; others saw it as wicked. Both groups fantasised, knowing little of that culture. Certainly China, unlike the West, was non-exploratory: wisdom met with a welcome there; nevertheless it found a target for oppression in such institutions as the binding of women's feet, together with other imprisoning measures. And a contempt for the happiness of women – a contempt admittedly to be found elsewhere, but always, where it was found, impeding a nobler culture. Yet China grew in economic strength.

The West, in those little cockleshell galleons of long ago, set out from Thames and Tiber, to gather knowledge or encourage conquest. Westerners, for one example, discovered the potato, an invaluable food crop, but, at the same time, the tobacco weed.

We may suppose that the early Ming dynasty invented the restaurant, that great gift to civilization. At its tables, guests might not only eat but could converse, exchanging scandal and ideas. The West seized late on this amenity where, with exceptions, it became linked with gluttony, and gluttony with obesity. And the hospitals of the West filled with underage drunkards. In the Islamic Middle East there were no drunkards, but no hospitals worthy of the name, little sanitation.

This is what we find so often, a move for the good, a slip to the bad. Kindness, kind acts, care, friendship are common, East or West; yet it is evil that hits the headlines. Are we drawn to evil, as a cat is to milk?

As there are gulfs between nations, so there are gulfs between rich and poor within a nation. As the populations of the world increase, so, exponentially, do the differences between economic prosperity and pauperdom. Whereas once the divisions between rich and poor, income-wise, were not great; now they grow wider yearly, even as Eastern countries such as India and China boast billionaires.

Some claim the British Empire was purely authoritarian. One sees today that countries such as Burma, freed from the British yoke, endured possession by a far greater tyranny. Even under the oppression of the Soviet Union and of Russia, those unfortunates escaping the cruel imposition of famine could feed themselves; whereas now, in countries such as Turkmenistan, their food comes from sources sponsored by UNICEF and UNESCO. Such well-intentioned systems merely increase inertia in the native population.

Most attempts to raise crop yields do not succeed. The planners who created canals drawing water from the Aral Sea merely destroyed the sea and poisoned the land around.

Attempts to improve Africa have been largely futile. The child soldier is still a symbol, despite the efforts of the twenty-first century. Tyranny, warfare, rape, starvation, illness, feature almost universally. Where women are chattels, little improvement can be expected. Where women are freer (as has happened only recently even in the West) some little improvement can be expected.

Overpopulation, water shortages, increase in the unproductive aged afflict both sexes.

Despite astonishing advances in, for one instance, medical science, there can be no general advance in humanity. We evolved from creatures whose objectives were to survive at all costs and to reproduce their own kind; despite grand buildings, grand speeches, even grand endeavours, these remain the predominant objectives. So we struggle. We flounder suffering diseases of the flesh and of corruption. We find little in the way of peace and contentment.

What conclusions can be drawn from this data? That this creature who has unsparingly overrun the planet deserves its self-inflicted misery?

We cannot improve. Matters will only get worse, are getting worse, until there comes some final catastrophe. We need to separate the truly enlightened from the vast majority. That can only be done by transplanting the best of our stock and striving – on Mars and beyond – to realise true civilization. Hardship, deprivation, may bring us a more continent and better humanity.

End

With thanks to Brendan Fleming for his encouragement

Brian W. Aldiss D.Litt., O.B.E.